Karmack

J.C. Whyte

MuseItUp Publishing
14878 James, Pierrefonds, Quebec, Canada, H9H 1P5

Cover Art © 2013 by Charlotte Volnek
Copyedited by Les Tucker
Layout and Book Production by Lea Schizas

Print ISBN: 978-1-77127-653-5
eBook ISBN: 978-1-77127-335-0
Production by MuseItUp Publishing

Praise for Karmack

"Karmack is a brilliant story."
—Mother Daughter Book Reviews

"Full of fun, fantasy, and fantastic revenge on a bully!"
—Shauna Wheelwright, I Love to Read and Review Books

"A great anti-bullying book; I highly recommend it."
—Bookworm Lisa Reviews

"Child-centered, non-preachy, and action-packed, it's a great classroom read-aloud."
—Carolyn Wilhelm, national board certified teacher, Wise Owl Factory

"Wonderfully entertaining...children ages 8-12...will love this book, especially boys."
—Paul R. Hewlett, author of the Lionel Snodgrass books

CHAPTER ONE

Creature on the Roof

"Let's get him," Sully said.

Breeze and Gonzo understood. Grabbing their backpacks, they followed Sully out the front door of the school. Sully was already locked on target—the kid looking over his shoulder, edging past the others waiting for buses.

This kid committed the most unforgiveable of crimes—he'd *told* on Sully! It happened in music class, when Mr. Gorsham asked who was making the fart sounds every time he started to play the piano. The squealer, who shall remain nameless, pointed to Sully. Then Mr. Gorsham took away Sully's whoopie cushion.

Now the squealer was about to get his just reward.

Sully, Breeze, and Gonzo pushed past the kids waiting for buses and ran down the long driveway of the school. The squealer was small but limber, easily jumping the rail fence at the Little League ballpark across the street.

His pursuers were not far behind. They too jumped the fence, bounded past the bleachers and headed out to left field. Although it was now April, a late-season snowfall in Western Pennsylvania had left mounds of caked ice and snow. This made it difficult for the boys to navigate the field.

Yet the squealer was jumping the far end of the fence, taking him out of the ballpark and across the street from the library. He was panting. His three pursuers, also panting, were still not far behind.

The squealer sped past the front of the library, narrowly missing a woman and her two children walking toward their car. Sully, Breeze, and Gonzo were only a few yards behind now. The woman saw the three approaching at full speed and pulled her kids back just in time. Sully had to swerve to avoid a collision. Gonzo came to a complete stop; then he went around the family. But Breeze flew right into the woman, almost knocking her to the ground.

"Hey, watch it," the woman shouted.

But Breeze only yelled, "Sorry," as he continued onward.

Now the squealer was at the soccer practice field, a wide open space with nowhere to hide. He started to panic. Could he make it to the trees or perhaps the houses across the road? Sully was nearly on his heels. And Breeze and Gonzo were right behind their leader.

Still running hard, the squealer screamed as loud as he could. But what good was that? The pursuers knew no one would come to this kid's rescue.

Then, just as Sully was about to grab him from behind, the squealer turned quickly to his right, running into the street. Though surprised, Sully adjusted to match this maneuver, turning just as quickly as the squealer. A few steps behind, Breeze and Gonzo didn't need to turn right—they just continued running.

His quick right turn bought the squealer a little bit of time, but not enough. So he tried the maneuver again and again, dodging and weaving his way into the downtown district. But this only made Sully angrier.

Through front yards, backyards, and down the main road, the pursuers continued to chase the squealer into town. Sully, Breeze, and Gonzo (also known as Curtis Sullenburg, Matthew Brezinski, and Carlos Gonzalez) were the toughest dudes in fifth grade. Everyone knew these three were definitely trouble. And the worst was Sully, their leader.

The old Statewide Bank building lay just ahead, on the corner of Main Street and Railroad Avenue. And that was where the squealer ran out of gas.

Sully immediately pinned him to the ground, right there at the corner. Lying in the snow, the squealer looked petrified. Sully laughed and let go of the boy—just knowing he scared the living daylights out of the kid was enough for Sully. But not Gonzo—he dropped his backpack on the left side of the squealer's face. "That's for making us chase you," he said.

Sully let out a loud "Hah!"

Then the boys heard a rumble. It came from above them—from the pitched roof of the bank. Sully looked up in time to see a bundle of snow drop from the roof. It fell downward, toward Gonzo, who was still hovering over the squealer.

"Hey, look out," Sully shouted, but not in time. Gonzo did look up, just as the pile of snow hit his face. The squealer managed to squirm out of the way and take off down the road. Breeze began to dig out his friend.

But Sully was frozen to his spot, still gazing at the roof of the bank. Because he saw something up there—a small figure no bigger than a two-year-old. And was it…*laughing?*

Sully knew it couldn't be a child. Not with that long, fat nose. Definitely not a child.

Was it just my imagination? Or maybe…a reflection…from ice on the roof? After giving his eyes a good rub, Sully changed his view of the roof by walking around the corner. And there—there was that little guy, laughing again! The creature in the funny green outfit saw Sully too. Then came a flash of light as it darted to the other side of the roof, beyond Sully's vision.

"Breeze…did you…see that?" Sully wanted to know.

"Yeah, Gonzo got dumped on. Lucky break for the squealer."

"No, I mean…ah, forget it." Sully knew he'd seen someone. Yet…

Never the shy one, Sully next ran into the bank to question the first teller he saw. "Is some guy up on the roof?"

"What?"

"You got some guy shoveling snow off the roof? My friend, he got dumped on."

"Uh, not that I'm aware of." The female teller turned around and asked the branch manager the same question. Then she returned to Sully. "No one's on the roof. What's the problem?"

"I saw…*somebody*…up there."

The manager came to the counter. "There's no one up there, son. Some snow must've fallen from the roof. Is your friend all right?"

"Yeah, I guess. But I coulda sworn I saw someone up there."

The teller smiled. "Probably just glare from the sun. Nice to have some sun today, huh?"

But Sully only shrugged and walked out of the bank.

The guys were waiting for him outside. Gonzo was dusty with snow. And he was cradling the left side of his face. It was red and starting to swell.

"What's going on?" asked Breeze.

"That's what I wanna know." Sully frowned as he committed the creature's face to his memory. Anyone crossing Sully usually lived to regret it.

That is…until now.

CHAPTER TWO

Second Encounter

Next day at school, everyone was laughing—about the snow falling on Gonzo. The squealer had told (could he keep his mouth shut about anything?).

When Sully entered the school building, he immediately saw the squealer trying to duck around a corner. The left side of the squealer's face was red and swollen from Gonzo's dropping his backpack on it. That made Sully smile. Then he saw Gonzo—he looked just like the squealer, his face red and swollen on the left side.

"Looks like you got hit by an avalanche," Sully said with a laugh.

"Not fummy," winced Gonzo. "It horts...even ta...awk."

Breeze joined the group. He too started to laugh when he noticed Gonzo's face.

"Not fummy," repeated Gonzo. "That snow hort."

The first bell rang and the fifth graders' day proceeded as usual, with the regular assortment of subjects, recess, another subject, and finally lunch.

Breeze, who'd been itching to taunt the new girl in their class, finally saw his chance. Vanessa was about to leave the cafeteria line with her tray of food. Breeze held a quick conference with Sully. When they separated, Breeze moved toward the girl and Sully walked up to the teacher whose turn it was to be lunch monitor.

"Hey, Mr. Robinson, you seen this?" Sully referred to some student artwork hanging on the cafeteria wall directly behind them.

The teacher spun around to see what the boy was pointing at. "What? You mean those pictures?"

"Yeah. Pretty good, huh?" Sully walked closer to a picture, in a deliberate attempt to divert the teacher's gaze from the cafeteria line.

"You interested in art, Curtis?"

The boy grimaced. He hated when teachers called him by his first name. *What tough guy is called Curtis?*

"Heck no," said Sully. He was telling the truth, yet was about to launch into an elaborate lie when SLAM! Vanessa's lunch tray hit the floor. Her food and drink flew everywhere. Yet Breeze was able to grab her slice of chocolate cake before it landed.

Both Sully and Mr. Robinson turned their heads in the direction of the disturbance. The teacher was about to go and investigate, but Sully needed to buy Breeze a little more time. So he said, "Hey! Mr. Robinson."

The teacher's head swiveled back. "What?"

Meanwhile, Breeze was sneering at the new girl and saying, "Welcome to Higgins Elementary, clumsy-butt!"

"Uh, never mind," said Sully.

The teacher turned and walked toward the cafeteria line. Sully grinned at the clean getaway. Breeze bumping that girl's tray was nothing new—just the typical stunt Sully and his gang pulled all the time. And usually got away with. As Sully headed back to his table, he could see Gonzo laughing his head off. Eight other boys were also at the table—the regular bunch of wannabes who hung around Sully's gang—and they were laughing too.

Breeze approached and, just as he was about to sit down in front of his food tray, a small leg suddenly pushed out from under the table. Sully could see it. And just like when the snow fell on Gonzo, there was no time for him to prevent what was about to happen.

Breeze's foot caught on the tiny leg and he lost his balance and fell onto the table, tipping one side of his tray. The contents of the tray flew up into the air; then came swiftly down, landing mostly on Breeze. There was linguine on his shirt, salad in his hair, and fruit cocktail dripping from his ear! The whole cafeteria erupted in laughter. Even Gonzo couldn't stop himself from laughing (although it *hort*).

But there was one kid not laughing. Sully. He was already under the table searching for the owner of that leg, the one that tripped Breeze. It was tiny, like the leg of a toddler. But it wasn't a child's leg, because it was full of dark, hairy stubble—the kind you'd see on an old man's leg. Sully suspected this leg belonged to the creature—the one he saw on the bank roof.

Weaving between the legs under the table, Sully didn't care who he was disturbing.

"Hey, whatcha doing?" Lucas had craned his neck under the table to see who was down there. But as soon as he spoke, Sully slapped the boy's face and continued on.

When he was satisfied the creature was no longer under the table, Sully came back up. "Any you punks seen that little guy?"

"What little guy?" asked Jake.

"The one who stuck his foot out to trip Breeze. About this tall." Sully held his hand two feet off the floor. "And oh yeah, he's got a big, fat nose."

The wannabes shifted their eyes at each other. They didn't know what to say.

"Aw c'mon," said Sully. "You musta seen him."

The boys' expressions now turned fearful. They knew to contradict their leader was just asking for trouble. "Uh…he musta got away," offered a brave soul.

Sully sulked for the remainder of the afternoon, angry that the creature had twice eluded him. *Gotta get that little...whatever he is!*

CHAPTER THREE

Gotcha!

With the arrival of April came after-school soccer practice for the town's travel teams. Sully, Gonzo, and Breeze were all on the Under-12 boys' team, so after school they walked the short distance to the practice field.

To warm up, the coach had them run some laps before the formal practice session. By their second lap around, Breeze noticed Sully was unusually quiet. "Something wrong, Sul?"

The boy slowed his pace to answer, but soon realized this was a mistake—Breeze's blond hair was still pungent with the odor of salad dressing. "Nah," said Sully. He didn't feel like talking to a stinky head.

Gonzo soon caught up to his friends. He was panting hard, his dark hair already glistening with sweat. "Bweeze…ten bucks… you can twip Bardo…without coach seeing." Bardo was what everybody called Anthony Lombardo, the team's goalkeeper. He was big for his age.

"No way! Last time I tried that, Bardo landed on top; nearly crushed me to death."

The reminder of that image made both Sully and Gonzo laugh. Then Sully said, "I'll do it. I could use the ten bucks."

So Sully sped up to catch Bardo. Within a few minutes, he was on the boy's heels. But at that moment, the coach blew his whistle, calling everyone in from the field. Sully had missed his chance to make an easy ten dollars. His sulk grew deeper. Soon he felt downright irritable. And when Sully was irritable, somebody usually got hurt.

The coach divided the boys into two lines in front of the goal. A boy from each line took a turn moving and kicking the ball toward the goal. As goalie, Bardo tried to keep the ball from making it past him and into the netting.

Sully, Breeze, and Gonzo stood together in the middle of the line to the right, awaiting their turns. Sully had an idea. "Hey, Gonz, you give me ten bucks if I smack Bardo below the belt?"

"Huh?"

"Ten bucks to land one in Ball Central Station."

"You're on!" said Gonzo.

As the line inched forward with each boy's kick, Sully eagerly waited for his turn. During the interval, he dug at the ground with the heel of his shoe. He did it again and again, harder each time. Sully knew he needed an outlet for his anger. His irritation had been mounting since lunch, when that creature had managed to escape him again. And who better to release anger on than Bardo. Especially if it also brought him a ten dollar bonus!

As he continued to wait, Sully could feel his legs itching to get moving. He wiggled one foot, and then the other, to loosen up his leg muscles. And then finally…it was his turn!

Sully positioned the soccer ball between his feet. The adrenaline was pumping, he could feel it. Moving the ball forward with his feet until he was in position to take a shot on the goal, Sully summoned forth all his strength. Then WHAM! He kicked that ball as hard as he could.

But the kick was too strong. Sully's shot soared over the top of the goal and bounded into the woods. All the kids laughed, especially Bardo. Sully was furious. His eyes became daggers as they targeted in on Bardo's wide, smiling face. He wanted to boot his cleated foot right into that face. *Worth getting into trouble for that*, he figured.

Yet the coach seemed to read Sully's mind. "Go get that ball," he ordered.

Sully punched his fist into the air; then he slogged into the woods. The ball had traveled farther than he thought. Although the forest floor was covered with fallen sticks and clumps of still-remaining snow, Sully could see the black-and-white soccer ball about fifty yards ahead. As he approached it, the boy also caught some movement out of the corner of his eye. Something small… and furtive. He turned quickly, but nothing was there. Just a brief flash of light. So Sully picked up the ball and returned to the soccer field.

When he got back, the team was divided into smaller groups, each running separate drills. And, for the moment, coach was busy instructing one of those groups. Sully realized this might be his last chance at releasing some of his anger.

Quietly, he sprinted up to Bardo's backside. Then he yelled, "Look out." As the goalkeeper spun around, Sully let him have it with the ball—right in the face!

"Owwwwww," screamed Bardo.

The players and coach all turned to see who was yelling.

But Sully said with a shrug, "The ball, it took a bad bounce."

Coach came up to Bardo. "You okay?" Holding his jaw, the boy waved him away.

Then out of nowhere, a huge gust of wind blew across the field. Everyone's hair flew straight upward. The gust was so strong, a tree branch high above cracked off from the trunk of the large oak nearby. Then another gust sent the branch in the direction of the boys on the field. Those standing next to Sully saw the branch coming and ran. But Sully was busy gloating over his victory, continuing to smirk at the grimacing goalkeeper. Bardo saw it coming too but refused to give a warning. So the branch landed right on top of Sully.

"Oh, man!" cried Gonzo as he rushed to his friend. Sully was splayed on the ground, holding his throbbing jaw. "You okay, Sul?"

The boy's head seemed to be spinning. But as his eyes regained their focus, Sully spied a small creature in green skipping along the edge of the woods. "That's him!" he shouted. Sully jumped up and headed for the woods.

His teammates looked startled; so did their coach.

Sully's friends were stunned too. "Should we go affer him?" Gonzo asked. Breeze didn't answer; he just stared after the boy disappearing into the woods.

Sully was determined to catch that creature. Deeper and deeper into the woods he ran, his eyes focused upon his prey. The creature was quick, yet its legs were short. *Just a matter of time…until I catch up. Then, kapowza!*

The creature zigged and zagged through the trees, moving so fast it sometimes became just a flash of light.

Yet Sully was fast too, and clever. He studied the creature's pattern and soon began to anticipate its moves. When he was within ten feet of the little guy, Sully knew the creature would next dart to its left, so he went in that direction. And sure enough, so did the creature! Sully surprised the little guy by appearing from around the side of a tree. "Gotcha!" he shouted.

CHAPTER FOUR

With the Creature

Sully and the creature wrestled on the ground for only a few moments. The creature seemed to realize that fighting a bigger, stronger opponent would be useless. So it shouted, "Leggo, leggo." And Sully mostly did. Yet he kept one hand clamped around the creature's wrist so it couldn't run off.

The boy sat down on a nearby log and pulled the creature before him to take a look at what he'd caught. He saw that it was exceedingly ugly, with a great bulbous nose, beady green eyes, and a very round midsection. Dark green hair sprouted like thick blades of grass from one spot on the top of its head. And its clothes, well…they were really just a bunch of leaves twisted together to form a sleeveless tunic. The creature's brownish arms and legs poked through the tunic like tree branches.

"You look like a little tree," concluded Sully. "But I know you ain't. What *are* you?"

As if resigning itself to the status of prisoner, the creature looked down and mumbled, "I's be karmic balancer."

Sully wasn't sure he heard right. "What?"

"Karmic…"

"Karmack? Your name's Karmack?"

The creature looked up while slowly turning its head from side to side. Seeking an escape route, perhaps?

Sully pulled it closer. "Okay, Karmack. I seen you—up on the roof yesterday, at the bank. And today—in the cafeteria, under the table."

The creature sighed. "You's must be speedy-eyed."

"Huh?"

"You's eyes must be speedy. I's too fast for most."

Sully raised his free hand to brush back a strand of dark brown hair that had fallen onto his forehead. Then he scratched his freckled nose. As he did, he realized his jaw was still throbbing from being whacked by that fallen branch. He gingerly rubbed the side of his face. "You…from outer space?" he finally asked.

That made the creature smile. A very broad smile, from pointy ear to pointy ear. But Sully could barely see how broad it was, what with the creature's long nose hanging out over its thin lips. "I's no from outer space."

"You talk funny. The way little kids talk."

The creature looked wary, but nodded. "I's be like little kid. You's…no hurt little kids?"

Sully smirked. "I do if they mess with me. You messing with me, Karmack?"

The creature winced. "I's job be balance. I's balance you's boys. 'Cause you's all outta balance."

"What are you talking about?"

"I's balance you's bad tricks. When bad tricks get too high, you's all outta balance. I's balance."

"Balance our bad tricks? What's that mean?"

"You's boys, make bad tricks. So I's give you's same you's do."

Sully squinted at the creature. He was starting to comprehend; well, maybe. "You mean, like when the snow dropped on Gonzo's face…after he dropped his backpack on the squealer? That was you…balancing him?"

" 'Xactly right! That boy, he's got hit in face for hit in face."

"Oh, man! You did that?"

"Be I's job."

"And when you tripped Breeze in the cafeteria…and his food went all over the place, just like what he did to the new girl…"

Karmack smiled at Sully.

"And just now…with the wind and the branch…after I smacked Bardo with the soccer ball…"

The creature took a little bow, even though Sully was still holding its wrist.

Sully grinned with newfound admiration. "Dude!"

"I *doed* it all right!" This Karmack was obviously proud of its accomplishments.

But Sully needed a few moments to mull over this amazing new information. Finally he said, "This…balancing thing you do. You do it…for everybody?"

"No, I's job be you's boys."

"Just me and my gang?"

" 'Xactly right."

"But why just us?"

"So many bad tricks. Too many. Pile high, over you's heads."

Sully immediately twisted his neck to look upward. "I don't see anything…"

"You's can no see. I's can see."

"What're you seeing?"

"Pile like skyscraper."

"A skyscraper?"

"Much high, over you's head. Bad tricks—all pile up…like skyscraper, over you's head."

Sully thought a moment. “And this is bad…to have a skyscraper over my head?”

“Very most bad. If I’s no balance, much danger for you’s.”

“Danger? What kind of danger?”

“Dreadful awful. Bad tricks, all pile up, mean something dreadful awful coming.”

“Something dreadful awful? Like what?”

“Like…” Karmack lightly tapped at the side of its head. “Ah, I’s found one. Last year, boy on you’s street. Dreadful awful bird attack.”

Sully knew immediately whom Karmack was referring to—Justin Berley, the kid who loved shooting at crows with his BB gun. Last summer, he got an eighteen-speed bike for his fourteenth birthday and immediately jumped on to try it. The boy rode down the street without a helmet, pedaling his bike while learning to shift the gears. But he was so engrossed with the shifting that he didn’t realize the bike was swerving off the road. It crashed right through the wire mesh of a neighbor’s pigeon coop. The birds went crazy, squawking and dumping poop all over him. When Justin finally emerged from the coop, he looked like the Abominable Snowman of pigeon poop. Worse yet, one of the wood perches had fallen onto his right hand, crushing the top of his trigger finger; his days of shooting at crows were over.

“Aw, c’mon. You expect me to believe you did that?”

“I’s no do. Boy’s skyscraper fall.”

“Yeah, but, why didn’t you balance him before that happened? Isn’t that your job?”

“I’s try. Boy make many bad tricks before I’s done. Too late—pile fall.”

Sully instinctively looked up, as if his own pile were about to topple. He frowned. “Man, Karmack, you got *some* power!”

“I’s no power. I’s worker.”

“Does everyone have this…pile…over his head?”

“All humans. But for most, not so high.”

"Mine's a skyscraper, you said."

"You's and you's friends."

"How'd our piles get so high?"

"More high with every bad trick."

"Bad tricks? You mean like the pranks we pull?"

"Mean tricks. Make hurt."

"Me and the guys, we pull pranks all the time. Just for… y'know, fun. No harm in that."

Karmack looked above Sully's head; then tapped the side of its own head. "I's see snake. In teacher's desk."

"Well, *that*. I was only a kid. In first grade, just getting started…"

"Teacher much scared. Heart almost stop."

Sully smiled at the delicious memory. "I remember."

Karmack again looked up and tapped its head. "Apples. You's boys drop on cars."

Again Sully smiled. "Yeah, but the branches were hanging over the road. Those apples woulda fallen on the cars even if we weren't up there, shaking the trees."

Another look up and another tap of the head. "Peanut butter. In tuna sandwich."

Sully assumed an innocent face for this one. "How was I to know Bradley was allergic?"

"He's go hospital."

"Well, he should come with a warning." The boy grinned. "You know, like animals at the zoo. A sign saying, don't feed peanut butter to this monkey." Then Sully amused himself by making what he considered to be excellent monkey sounds.

Once more, Karmack looked upward and tapped. "Worms. Front seat, teacher's car."

"Yeah, well, Trembley shouldn't have given so much homework over that holiday weekend. He deserved what he got."

Another look up and a tap. "Punches. Many, many punches. Other boys."

"They all deserved what they got."

"Many bad tricks, pile high."

Sully became quiet as he mulled over what he'd just learned. *This little dude, guess he's gonna keep balancing me every time I pull a prank.* The boy rubbed his sore jaw. *Man, I gotta do something about this!* He had an idea. "Hey, Karmack, I know lots of guys who need balancing. I could like, point them out. Then you'd have lots of balancing to do."

"I's job be you's boys…"

"Yeah, but you're missing the bigger picture here. You probably don't realize it, but fifth grade is *full* of guys like me, pulling pranks. So why limit yourself to just me and my friends? If we joined forces, you and me could like, *own* this town. Whattayasay? Friends?"

Karmack's green eyes looked furtively to the left and right. Sully thought the creature might still be thinking of escape. But instead it asked, "How…we's be friends?"

"Well, y'know…by helping each other. Like, I'll find guys… who need balancing…and point 'em out to you. Then you can balance 'em, see?"

The creature hesitated. Was that fear Sully smelled? Then, with its free hand, Karmack pointed to its wrist. "Friends? I's be gotcha."

"Huh? *Gotcha?*"

"You's say 'gotcha' when grab. I's be gotcha."

Sully had to laugh. "Yeah, that's right. But sometimes 'gotcha' means you *get* something, like you understand. So if you understand I caught you, then you're gotcha that I gotcha. Get it?"

"I's gotcha…*and* I's be gotcha?"

"Exactly." Sully let go of the creature's pudgy little arm. "Y'know, Karmack, we could make a great team—me finding kids needing balance—and you whacking 'em." Sully pictured the creature tying up Bardo in the netting of the soccer goal; then him kicking the ball directly at the goalkeeper. *Gooooooooooooal!*

When Sully came back to earth, he gave Karmack a more serious look. "Just one thing, though. How'll I reach you? I mean, you ain't got a cell phone or anything, do ya?"

"No phone."

"Then how's this gonna work? I gotta point out guys to whack…I mean balance."

"I's see all things with you's and you's friends. I's job to watch and balance."

"Oh, right. So you'll see me point…or maybe nod toward some kid? And you'll understand what I mean…right?"

"Gotcha!" the creature said excitedly.

"Y'know, when you say it like that, 'gotcha' means you pulled a joke on someone."

"A joke? For…laugh?"

"Yeah, for laughs. Like if I stuck out my foot and you tripped over it. I'd laugh and say, 'gotcha!' Know what I mean?"

"Gotcha," said the creature.

"Okay, well, we got ourselves a deal now. So put 'er there." Sully stuck out his hand. But Karmack had no idea what to do with it. So the creature spit in the open palm.

"Hey! Whadja do that for?" But Sully's irritation was short-lived as a thought occurred to him. "That how you little guys… y'know, make a deal on…whatever planet you're from?"

"Gotcha," repeated Karmack.

The boy wiped his hand on the side of his pants. "So…we start tomorrow. I'll begin pointing kids out when I get to school. I know you'll be around, Karmack. You won't have to show yourself." He rose to leave. "By the way, my name's Sully."

"Gotcha," said Karmack again.

Sully started back to the practice field. Karmack watched him go. When he got about a hundred yards away, the boy turned to look back. Karmack was still standing there, watching. Sully gave two thumbs up; then he ran off.

Once outside the woods, the boy leapt into the air, excited by his deal with the creature. Yet…could he count on this Karmack? Or would the creature pull a *gotcha?*

CHAPTER FIVE

Whackings

That night, Sully lay awake in bed, imagining the mischief he would create with his new buddy, Karmack. He was also compiling a list in his head—a list of the kids he wanted whacked and the order of their whackings. Bardo was definitely first. Especially after the way he laughed at Sully's shot that flew over the goal.

Of course, not everyone on the list would get whacked out of revenge. Some would get it out of general principle. Like Nate Thomas, smartest kid in fifth grade—he had to get whacked for that. And Regina Pappadorocious deserved a whacking just for her ridiculously long name. And there were a bunch of kids Sully simply wanted to prank. So the list grew and grew.

He was thinking too, maybe when Karmack was finished whacking kids, he could then do teachers. Sully had a long list of those he'd like to see whacked. Best part was, nobody'd even know he was behind the whackings. Could life get any sweeter than that?

Morning came and Sully was raring to go. He practically flew out of bed, threw some clothes on, gulped down his cereal, ran a comb through his hair, slid his backpack over one shoulder, and galloped down the street.

Since he lived only three blocks from school, Sully got there in no time at all. But it was barely 8 a.m. Teachers were still parking their cars and entering the building. They saw Sully standing at the back door, grinning like the cat that ate the canary. Mr. Robinson looked surprised as Sully opened the door for him.

"Morning, Curtis. Aren't you a bit early?"

"No sir!" Sully mockingly saluted the teacher. Mr. Robinson just shrugged and marched down the hall toward his classroom. *Let me think now—number fifteen on the teacher's list*. Then came some more teachers. Sully continued to hold open the door and greeted each in turn with a salute. *Number seven, number eighteen, number two*. He had a good memory for numbers.

About twenty teachers later, Sully was tired of holding the door open and headed for his classroom. Along the way, he looked out the corners of his eyes, aware that Karmack could be lurking just about anywhere. Around any corner. In any classroom. And because Sully was—what did Karmack call it? Oh yeah, *speedy-eyed!* Because he was speedy-eyed, he was bound to spot that critter eventually.

As Sully waited in his classroom, students began to stagger in. Most seemed half asleep. Yet not Sully. He was more alert—and cheerful—than ever, greeting each student in turn. "Hey, Stefan." "How ya doing, Kyle?" "Say there, Christine."

Finally, Gonzo and Breeze came in together. Sully hadn't told them about his meeting with Karmack yet. He wanted to surprise them with his amazing new power of whacking people without lifting a finger. "Hey, buds!" said Sully.

Gonzo looked at him and grunted. But Breeze asked, "What're *you* so happy about?"

"Well, it's a great day, ain't it?"

"No, it ain't," Breeze said rather gruffly. "Got a math test after lunch. Remember?"

This didn't damper Sully's spirits. Because he believed something great would happen before then. Something… *Karmack!* But at this moment, Sully was still waiting for the person at the top of his list—Bardo, the one with the supreme honor of being first to get whacked.

And then, in walked the goalkeeper!

"Watch this," Sully told Breeze and Gonzo. Then he pointed directly at Bardo from about ten feet away. Nothing happened. So Sully moved closer. He pointed again, from about five feet away. Again, nothing.

I must be doing something wrong. Or else Karmack's taking a coffee break. "Karmack," Sully whispered as he looked around the room. "Psst, Karmack!"

Gonzo came up from behind. "Who you talking to, Sul?"

"Huh? Ain't talking to nobody. Just myself."

"Well, that's a new one. I never seen you talking to yourself before."

As Sully again pointed to Bardo, his target began to notice. "Why you pointing at me?"

Assuming his tough guy face, Sully rolled his hand into a fist. "I can point at you if I want to!"

This prompted Bardo to raise his hands, palms forward, as he retreated backward. "Didn't mean nothing by it," he said.

"Yeah well…you'd better not." Sully felt his temperature rising. *Where's that Karmack?*

Some girls were chatting beside him. Out of habit, Sully knocked a book from the hands of the closest girl. But because of the force he used, the book flew into a science project placed on a nearby desk. The impact tipped over several of the glued pieces in the model.

"Hey," cried Molly when she saw what he'd done to her science project. But Sully only laughed; he loved pulling stunts that got an immediate reaction.

Moments later, Sully saw his own history book lift from his desk and miraculously fly across the room. It landed on top of his science project, already placed on a side table with some others. And of course, several glued pieces were knocked loose.

Sully looked quickly around the room. And there, trying to slip through a slightly opened window, was...Karmack!

Pushing the girls aside, Sully raced to the window. The creature had nimbly squeezed itself through; then slammed the window shut just as the boy reached it. Sully lifted the window and forced himself out, falling hard onto the earth below.

When he looked up, he saw Karmack running full out, zigging and zagging like before. But occasionally the creature seemed to disappear and be replaced by flashes of light; this made it hard to follow with any human eye.

Yet Sully assumed Karmack was headed for the woods—that safe haven where the creature could blend in with branches and trees. The boy picked up his speed. And right before Karmack had the chance to reach the safety of the woods, Sully nabbed him.

Ooooomph. Karmack hit the ground. Sully straddled the creature's belly while pinning its arms down with his hands.

"What's the big idea?" the boy demanded. "I oughta beat the crap outta you."

Terror flashed in Karmack's eyes. "I's be like little kid! Please, no hurt little kid!"

Begging always seemed to soften Sully. He let go of the creature's arms. But he continued to straddle its belly, and thrust a fist at its fat nose. "All right, you got some explaining to do. And I ain't getting up until you do."

Karmack nodded its head. "I's job be balance, only you's and you's friends. I's...got no power for more. No power."

"You *do* have power," argued Sully. "I seen it with my own eyes. You made my book fly across the room."

Karmack tried to explain. "I's got no choice. I's job be balance you's and you's friends only."

Sully studied the pitiful creature below him. Since it looked so scared, he decided it was probably telling the truth. "Okay, but you gotta explain this whole business…better than that."

"I's…promise. Explain whole business, better."

"You won't try and escape?"

"I's promise. I's stay here…explain whole business, better."

Sully grunted as he rolled off the little guy. He searched for a log to sit on, all the while keeping a close eye on his captive. Once Sully settled himself, Karmack got up and stood directly in front of him.

"I's tool," the creature began. "I's do what universe says. Some humans need balance, I's must balance."

"That all you do? Go around the world…balancing people?"

The creature shook its head. "I's nature spirit, got much jobs. Only now, I's job be balance you's boys. On accounta you's be so outta balance."

"I get that. But what's a…nature spirit?"

"Nature spirit moves nature. How you's think earthquakes shake…hurricanes blow… volcanoes explode? Be nature spirit's job."

"But…who tells you to do those things?"

The creature shrugged. "Just…universe."

"The *universe?* How's the universe communicate with you?"

Karmack shrugged again. "I's get message," the creature said while tapping its head, "up here."

"So…are there more nature spirits, or are you the only one?"

"Many, many. I's be one of many, many."

"Okay, but…people can't *see* nature spirits. Can they?"

"'Xactly right! We's so speedy!"

"But *I* see you…"

"Most unusual. Happen sometime…human who can see. Like I's told you's—the speedy-eyed. On accounta you's speedy-eyed, you's can see nature spirit do job."

Sully had no idea such spirits even existed. And just think—he was one of the few who could see them. "Karmack, my man, I think I understand. But why'd you make a deal with me the other day? You know, to whack the kids I point out?"

"I's no can. But you's hurt…if I's say no."

Sully nodded. It was a reason he'd heard plenty of times before. "So you still gonna whack me…when I prank somebody?"

"Prank?"

"Yeah, like today—when I knocked that book outta Christine's hands. That was just a prank. Meant to be funny. Not to hurt anybody. You see the difference?"

"I's no see. You's make bad tricks, I's balance. You's remember skyscraper?"

He remembered. "What exactly would happen to me—if, y'know, my skyscraper fell?"

"Dreadful, awful doom. Change you's life. You's no want. I's save you's and you's friends."

Sully sighed and shook his head. He was beginning to feel more like a prisoner than this captive before him. "There's gotta be a better way to get balanced, Karmack. I know you're just trying to help and all, but I don't wanna keep getting whacked."

Karmack smiled. "You's speedy-eyed *and* speedy-smart. There much better way be balance—you's make good tricks!"

"Huh? I gotta do *nice* stuff?"

" 'Xactly! Like scale, you's pile one side with good tricks, balance side with bad tricks. But you's need make many good tricks, balance skyscraper."

Sully frowned. "*Many* good tricks? That'd kill me, Karmack."

"You's can make."

Sully cringed at the thought of what this would involve. "So you're saying, I gotta be some goody two-shoes."

Karmack looked a little puzzled. "You's no need shoes. Just make good tricks. So can balance bad. You's be kind, you's smile, and…" The creature trailed off.

"Yeah? And what else?"

Karmack winced a little. "And…no punches."

"That all, huh? Just be some wimpy dude who doesn't punch people, even when they need it." Sully picked up a stick and pitched it into the ground. "Know what I am, Karmack? The Big Cheese. The guy everyone looks up to. I waited my whole life—all these years in elementary school. Now I'm finally in fifth grade and get to be the Big Cheese. But to *stay* the Big Cheese, you gotta be tough. You need to keep the other guys in line, make 'em show some respect. Know what I mean? You gotta have respect if you wanna stay the Big Cheese."

"You's…Big Cheese?"

"None bigger. And guys, they respect me. 'Cause if they don't, I clobber 'em."

"Big Cheese clobber 'em?"

Sully pitched the stick into the ground again. "Yeah. See, I got a reputation to uphold. Can't do that by being a nice guy."

"Big Cheese…no nice guy?"

"Listen, Karmack, next fall I start middle school where only an eighth grader gets to be the Big Cheese. That's three years away for me. So when I start sixth grade, I gotta already have some respect to build on. So that by eighth grade, I can be the Big Cheese again. Being a nice guy only gets in the way of that."

Karmack's little green eyes shifted back and forth in their sockets. Eventually, the creature replied, "But…you's be nice guy, I's no need balance you's."

Sully sighed and flipped the stick over his shoulder. “Okay. If I’m good, you’ll go away and leave me alone? No more balancing?”

Karmack nodded.

“Guess I could…just, y’know, threaten guys. Promise to punch ‘em without actually doing it. That’d work, huh? I could still act tough, and not hit anybody. But…don’t ask me to *smile* —tough guys don’t smile.”

This made Karmack smile. “Gotcha!”

“Huh? Whattayamean by that?”

“Gotcha!” The creature continued to smile.

“You have no idea what that means, do ya?”

“Gotcha!”

Now Sully was the one who didn’t understand. He put out his hand to shake on their new deal, momentarily forgetting what Karmack had done the last time he did that. Sully quickly retracted his hand as the creature leaned forward to spit. “Gotcha,” said the boy. Then he took off.

The creature was still smiling as he left, perhaps hoping things would be different now. Yet part of Karmack’s job was to wait and see.

CHAPTER SIX

Keeping out of Trouble

Sully was feeling pretty good as he walked back to his classroom. *I'm in control of my destiny*, he told himself. *All I gotta do is stay outta trouble and remember not to clobber guys. How hard can that be?*

But just as Sully was about to enter the school's front entrance, he spied a caterpillar on the ground nearby. It was black and extremely furry. He picked the critter up and put it in his pocket; now he had something to play with during English class.

It was 8:40 a.m. and the students were beginning to look more awake. The first bell had rung and all the students were taking their seats. Sully glanced over at Gonzo, just two rows away. He pulled out the furry caterpillar and held it in the air. Gonzo smiled, thinking Sully had some devious plan; he continued to watch.

Sully then turned his attention to Breeze, sitting on the other side of the room. When Breeze saw the caterpillar, he also smiled, thinking the same thing as Gonzo.

Their teacher, Ms. Komplin, entered the room. "Morning, everyone." And the day began with her giving some school announcements and reminders. Sully was only half-listening. He'd put the caterpillar on his desk and was watching it inch along to the edge. When it got there, he turned it around to crawl back the other way.

Seated in the desk in front of Sully was Abigail Arbitter. Sully thought she was a particularly silly girl. A girly-girl, who jumped every time she saw any kind of bug. Now he wondered what Abigail would do if he held the caterpillar to the back of her neck. Would she know it was a caterpillar? Would she scream? He had to find out.

Sully placed the furry back of the caterpillar against Abigail's neck.

The girl involuntarily jumped in her seat. Then she spun around to find out what had just touched her. But Sully had already replaced the caterpillar in his pocket. He gave her a look that said *What's the matter with you?* Abigail continued to stare at him a few seconds more, looking closely at his hands and desk. Seeing nothing out of the ordinary, she rubbed her neck to make sure nothing was there. Satisfied, she turned back around.

Sully covered his mouth with a hand to keep his laugh from escaping. Gonzo did the same. Breeze glanced over, but he was too far away to be able to tell what was going on. Yet Breeze kept his eyes on Sully so he wouldn't miss any of the fun.

Taking the caterpillar from his pocket, Sully once more placed it up against the back of Abigail's neck. And just like before, the girl responded by turning quickly around. She glared at Sully. The boy scarcely had time to curl the caterpillar up in his hand.

"*What're you doing?*" she demanded in a loud whisper so Ms. Komplin wouldn't hear.

But Sully put on his most innocent-looking face, shrugging his shoulders in one big motion. Abigail couldn't see the caterpillar in his curled-up fist. "Nothing, ain't doing nothing."

Abigail narrowed her eyes at him. "You leave me alone, Curtis Sullenburg."

"Shhh!" responded Sully. "I'm trying to hear Ms. Komplin."

"Yeah, right," said the girl.

"Abigail?" the teacher asked. "You have something you'd like to share with the class?"

The girl spun back around. "Um, no, Ms. Komplin. I just… thought I felt something…on my neck."

"On your neck?"

"It was…fuzzy."

"Fuzzy?"

A few students started to titter.

"It…it's nothing. I guess." Abigail gave up. And the teacher moved on.

Sully and Gonzo were about to bust a gut. They were laughing so hard, yet trying not to make a sound. Abigail heard them and knew something was up. But she assumed Sully was touching her with some piece of fabric. She resolved to ignore it; she wasn't about to give this boy the reaction he wanted.

But since Sully was Sully, he wouldn't let it go. Taking the caterpillar from his curled-up first, the boy again laid it against Abigail's neck. The girl felt the furry substance and gritted her teeth. The teacher was droning on about the upcoming field trip, and Abigail was not about to interrupt her again.

Sully was disappointed not to get a reaction this time. So he moved the caterpillar along the back of the girl's neck, as if it were crawling on its own. Abigail now realized this was not just some fabric—*it was a creepy crawly critter!* Her body jerked unexpectedly, knocking the caterpillar loose from Sully's hand. And it dropped down the back of Abigail's shirt.

Oh, man! Am I in for it now.

Abigail felt the caterpillar on her back. "*Aiiiiiiiiiie,*" the girl screamed as she jumped from her desk. She wiggled her body and desperately tried to reach down inside the back of her shirt.

Ms. Komplin's eyes were wide as she asked, "What's wrong, Abigail?"

"Something's…in my shirt! He…"—she pointed at Sully—"he dropped something down my back! And I feel it… *crawling.*"

All the girls in the classroom found this news horrifying, as they gasped and clutched their throats. The boys, however, were laughing hysterically. That is, all but Sully. He was busy trying to explain to Ms. Komplin that he didn't mean to do it. The teacher then told Abigail to go to the girls' washroom and remove whatever it was crawling up her back. Lily volunteered to go with her, saying she wasn't afraid to touch a bug. The two girls practically flew out of the room.

Ms. Komplin's full attention was now on Sully.

"Honest, I didn't mean it, Ms. Komplin. She jerked… bumped my hand. I didn't mean to do it…"

And of course that was the truth. But when you're a known prankster, you're not likely to be believed. Sully was told to report for detention at the end of the day.

But that wasn't the worst part—Sully realized that Karmack might not understand either.

CHAPTER SEVEN
Completely Buggy

Sully spent the rest of the morning on edge, jumping at even the slightest noise or disturbance. He imagined that Karmack was right there next to him. About to fling a giant caterpillar down his shirt.

"Whatsamatter, dude?" asked Gonzo as he and Sully got their jackets for recess. Sully looked at him like a man possessed. His eyes were bulging and his forehead showed beads of sweat. Sully always seemed a bit wired to Gonzo. But not usually this much.

"You see something coming my way…you'll let me know, won't ya?" Sully asked him.

"Huh? Like what?"

"*Anything!*"

It shocked Gonzo to see the toughest kid in school so nervous. "Ah…sure, Sul. I got your back." But he looked over at Breeze as if to say, *weird, man.*

Sully was sure it would come. Whatever it was Karmack…or the universe…had determined to inflict on him. It would come. He just knew it.

When lunchtime arrived, Breeze and Gonzo sprinted to the cafeteria. But Sully held back. Lunch would be the perfect opportunity for Karmack to strike. All the commotion at the tables, the noise, and laughter—perfect for Karmack to race in unnoticed and drop something on Sully. "I'm skipping today," he told his friends.

Breeze laughed. "You on a diet?"

Sully scowled at him.

"Just a joke, man. Geesh, you're so…like…*sensitive* lately."

"Am not," argued their once-fearless leader.

"You are, Sul," agreed Gonzo. "Something's eating at you. I can tell."

"Beat it, you two!"

When his friends left, Sully considered where would be a good place to hide. *Inside a janitor's closet? Nah, too uncomfortable. The boys' washroom? Hmmm. Prob'ly too stinky*. Then he remembered the school's courtyard, an open-air square just off the cafeteria. It was an enclosed spot, bounded on four sides by the cafeteria, two classrooms, and the library. That meant Karmack would probably have to come over the roof to get at him.

But the courtyard, which featured a cherry tree and picnic tables, was not yet open. School administration always waited until the weather was warm enough for students to take their lunches outside. Although this day was reasonably warm, it was the first such day of the year. And apparently, administration was waiting for consistently warm weather. So the door to the courtyard was locked.

Undeterred, Sully decided to enter through one of the classrooms bordering the courtyard. He soon found one with an open window. And no one was there. He closed the classroom door; then he raced to the window. He climbed through and dropped into the courtyard.

It was very peaceful there. A few birds were fluttering about the cherry tree already starting to bloom. Sully found the spot he had in mind—at the base of the tree. He sat on the cold ground and leaned back against the trunk. "Ahhhhhhh." Now Sully could relax, protected by the walls all around him. Plus, he had a good line of sight for anything coming his way.

The spot was so peaceful, so quiet. And Sully was feeling tired. All that anxiety over Karmack whacking him had completely drained the boy. The lids of his eyes started to wilt; they didn't want to stay open. He was feeling so tired, so drowsy. And soon, Sully was fast asleep.

But not for long. Karmack was there. In the cherry tree, sitting beside a flat, white nest strung between two branches. Actually, it wasn't a bird's nest at all. It was a nest of tent caterpillars.

Karmack knew what he had to do. He started shaking the cherry tree. Hard. Soon, handfuls of baby caterpillars began dropping from their nest. Dropping. Onto Sully. Handfuls and handfuls. It was a big nest. But the boy continued to nap even as the small caterpillars crawled on his head and shirt. Finally, Karmack broke off a twig and used it to dislodge the nest. When it fell onto Sully's head, that was finally enough to rouse the boy.

He woke with a start. "Wha…?" That's when he felt them, crawling all over—especially on his head. "Aiiiiiiiiiiiiiii!" Sully jumped up and tried to brush the caterpillars off. He jumped some more.

A student sitting next to a cafeteria window noticed the jumping boy. "Hey look! It's Sully. And he's…*dancing?*"

Other kids raced for the windows. Several pointed at the near-hysterical Sully. Someone snickered. Then another. Soon everyone was jockeying for position at the windows. And all were laughing—at the school's most notorious bully.

The cafeteria monitor—still Mr. Robinson—came over to investigate. He couldn't believe what he saw: Sully jumping, wiggling, and pulling caterpillars out of his hair.

"How'd Curtis get out there?" the teacher asked.

"Dunno," answered Bardo, laughing the hardest. "But he's putting on a good show!"

Mr. Robinson wasn't laughing. "Madison," he directed the girl standing next to him, "go down to administration and get the key to the courtyard. I need to rescue a student who's definitely headed for detention."

* * * *

"Man. Double-dee!"

His head still dripping from the washroom sink, Sully didn't appreciate Gonzo stating the obvious. Yeah, he got double detention. The first for dropping a caterpillar down Abigail's back. For that, Ms. Komplin made Sully clean out the hamster's cage at the end of the day. It was a stinky job, but at least he liked the rodent.

Uma Shasthri, a girl from India whose father was attending graduate school in the area, had stayed after to work on her science project. She smiled at Sully. "Karmic caterpillar," she told him.

The boy stopped cleaning the cage. "You mean you see Karmack too?"

"See karma? No one really *sees* karma."

"No…Karmack. I thought you said the little guy's name."

"What little guy?"

"Nevermind—what were *you* talking about?"

"Karma. It's the Hindu belief that what you do in life comes back to you. Both the good and the bad. Those caterpillars dropping on your head? Perhaps you were getting paid back for what you did to Abigail."

"But that was just an accident. She bumped the caterpillar outta my hand."

Uma smiled knowingly. "Uh-huh—karma."

Sully's second detention was for sneaking into the locked courtyard. For that, Mr. Robinson made Sully sweep up the debris out there. As he swept, his mind drifted to thoughts of revenge.

Sully rightly assumed Karmack was behind the caterpillar episode. And he was especially angry at being "balanced" when he never intended to drop that caterpillar down the girl's shirt. *How come an accident counted as a bad trick? Bad trick? Hey, I'm starting to sound just like Karmack. Man, when I get my hands on that little creep…*

But how could he? Karmack only made an appearance when balancing someone. Sully certainly wanted no more of that.

And yet…since Karmack also balanced Breeze and Gonzo, perhaps Sully didn't need to put *himself* at risk. There was an idea!

But in order to trap the little guy, Sully knew he needed to be crafty. He couldn't just tell Breeze or Gonzo to pull a prank. Because Karmack might see him give the order. No, Sully would have to be more…subtle—he'd have to *inspire* his guys to come up with a prank on their own.

Yet this wouldn't be easy. Breeze wasn't all that bright, and neither was Gonzo. They relied on Sully to be the brains of their operation. So how could he get them to pull a prank without giving a direct order?

Then Sully remembered something: these guys despised Bardo as much as he did.

CHAPTER EIGHT

Rules of the Game

The travel team had soccer games scheduled for every Saturday through mid-June. On the Saturday of their first home game, Sully met up with Breeze and Gonzo on the soccer field.

"That Bardo!" said Sully as they watched their goalkeeper going through his warm-up exercises. "I'd sure like someone to teach him a lesson."

"Huh?" said the always-clueless Breeze.

"What kind of lesson?" asked the almost-as-clueless Gonzo.

"The kind," replied their sly leader, "that would teach him to show some respect. Bardo thinks he's so tough. He needs to be brought down a few notches. Know what I mean?"

Gonzo and Breeze needed some time to think about that. Yet Sully was sure his words would inspire them to act.

As the game got underway, the boys took their positions on the field. Because of his naturally aggressive nature, Sully was one of three strikers and he usually ended up scoring most of the team's goals. Breeze and Gonzo were defenders, playing the backfield on either side of the goal. They were the last line of defense before the ball got to Bardo.

The game proceeded along, with each team scoring a goal in the first half. But right before second half, Sully saw Breeze and Gonzo whispering to each other on the sidelines. Sully rubbed his hands together—perhaps something interesting was on the horizon.

Sully was right. After the second half began, a midfielder for the opposing team began moving the ball down the center of the field toward the goal. Gonzo nodded at Breeze and smiled. Then as the midfielder passed the ball to his striker, Gonzo and Breeze ran at the goal as if defending it. But instead, they each slammed into a side of Bardo, throwing the boy off balance. Bardo landed hard on his backside, having had the wind knocked out of him. The striker then tapped the ball into the netting of the undefended goal. The visiting team cheered.

Sully and his teammates moaned; their coach threw up his arms.

What were these guys thinking, wondered Sully? *I shoulda known better than to trust these imbeciles to handle something on their own.*

Yet Sully had achieved what he'd hoped for—his pals had pulled off what Karmack called a bad trick. But where *was* that little guy? Sully surveyed the field—no sign of Karmack yet. But he'd continue to keep a lookout. Because there was bound to be some balancing.

Meanwhile, play had resumed on the soccer field. Sully's team failed to score a goal on their next attempt and the visiting team regained possession of the ball. As a midfielder kicked the ball to a striker, Breeze and Gonzo moved forward to defend. The striker lined up his shot, but it took a funny bounce and smacked right into Gonzo's midsection. The boy fell backward into Breeze, who was right behind him. They both landed hard on their backsides, having had the wind knocked out of them.

Sully's eyes grew wide. That Karmack was around somewhere. But…*where?*

Bardo managed to get the ball and kick it to the opposite end of the field. Sully then trapped the ball with his feet and began to drive to the goal. But as he did, he saw some flashes out of the corner of one eye. A quick glance to the side revealed Karmack zig-zagging toward the woods.

Desperate to catch the varmint, Sully passed up an open shot on the goal and instead kicked the ball to a surprised teammate. Then he took off for the woods. After the other striker scored a goal, the players on the field all stopped to watch Sully, running at top speed toward the woods.

"Hey," said an opposing player, "don't that kid know the porta potties are the other way?"

But Sully was on a mission. And he wasn't about to stop until Karmack was once more in his hands. Just inside the woods, he caught up to the creature.

"No hurt," Karmack pleaded as Sully grabbed hold of its neck. "No hurt…!"

"I *am*…gonna hurt," Sully said, panting. He looped his arm around the little guy's neck.

"But…I's no hurt you's. I's only balance."

"And you think that don't hurt?"

"I's hurt you's?"

The fire was still in Sully's eyes, but he loosened his grip a little. "'Course you hurt me."

"I's only balance."

"But you hurt me when I don't deserve it. That's not fair."

The creature looked puzzled. "I's…just give what you's give. No more."

"That's not true! I got a whole nest of caterpillars dumped on me, and all I did was *accidentally* drop one down a girl's shirt. I got a whole lot more than I gave!"

Karmack remained silent a moment. Was the creature considering what Sully had said? Finally it replied, "Job no perfect." Karmack now looked pathetic and this seemed to soften Sully again.

Letting go of its neck, Sully shook his head at the creature. "Don't you know the difference between doing something mean, and stuff that's a joke…or an accident?"

Again Karmack seemed puzzled. "Accy…dent?"

"Yeah. Like when something that wasn't supposed to happen, happens. And you didn't want it to. You know, like when your job *no perfect*. You understand me?"

Karmack nodded. "Gotcha. Accy-dent."

"Sometimes my gang, we do things just for a joke. To give everyone a good laugh."

"Laugh be good. But I's see no laugh in you's skyscraper. Only hurt."

"Okay, well…sometimes people don't *get* our jokes. Y'know? But they're still jokes. You gotta understand that difference before you go balancing…and hurting me and my guys."

Karmack's eyes were bright and eager, and Sully thought perhaps it was trying to understand. "Difference be…some bad tricks…just be laugh?"

"Yeah. Exactly. Someone shoulda explained that, before you were sent to balance us."

But then Karmack seemed to reconsider. "Caterpillar. No laugh. She's cry."

Sully scowled. "Yeah well, that's because she's a girl." He shook his head. "You wouldn't understand."

"She's hurt. She's cry."

The boy showed his open palms to the creature. "But I didn't *mean* to hurt her…"

"You's take caterpillar from ground?"

"Well, yeah…"

"You's put caterpillar on neck?"

"I was just joking around…"

"Caterpillar fall in she's shirt?"

The boy couldn't help but smile while remembering the sight of Abigail jumping and wiggling about.

"You's laugh; she's no laugh. You's make bad trick."

Sully blinked at the creature. Obviously, his argument wasn't making any headway. So the boy went to his default position, the one which always worked when logic failed. "Look, Karmack, let me explain the rules of the game to you. You keep punishing me for stuff that's accidents and jokes, and I'm gonna have to come back and clobber you."

"Cla…clawber I's?"

"Yeah, I'm gonna have to hurt you."

Karmack instinctively took a step backward. "You's *hurt* I's?"

"Don't wanna. But you keep this up, I'm coming back. And I'll catch you…"

"I's…only balance."

Sully felt his temperature rising. "Well, it ain't your job to make me pay for something that ain't mean. And that's what you been doing! So lay off, or…" Sully rolled his hand into a fist and put it in Karmack's face. The little creature's eyes grew to the size of saucers.

The boy sneered. "I'm giving you fair warning, Karmack, something I don't give most guys who cross me. But I'm warning you—find another job or I'll make sure you become permanently unemployed. Got it?"

That was enough to make the creature take off. Sully saw flashes of light through the trees until Karmack completely disappeared from view.

When the boy returned to the soccer field, his friends wanted to know what was up.

"Didn't you see him? That little green and brown guy?"

"A little...green and brown guy...?" Gonzo repeated.

"A leprechaun?" asked Breeze.

Sully knew it was a waste of breath with these two. Maybe the next time he caught Karmack, he'd bring the creature back to show them.

The coach, however, didn't want to hear any excuse for Sully's leaving in the middle of a play. He made Sully sit on the sidelines for the rest of the game. So of course their team lost.

Yet, thought Sully, if he and Karmack had finally come to an understanding, then losing the game was worth it. Because being held responsible for an accident simply wasn't fair.

Especially since accidents always seemed to happen around Sully and his gang.

CHAPTER NINE

Accidents Happen

Eva Jaworski was whimpering at her desk. Ms. Komplin had been in the middle of an English lesson, putting sentences on the dry-erase board for diagramming, when the girl whispered something to Ruthanne Reilly. Ms. Komplin heard a low voice and turned to catch her in the act; then she put the girl's name on the detention list in the top right corner of the board.

Now Sully was finding it hard to concentrate due to Eva's whimpering. The girl sniffed and sniffed, gagged a little, and occasionally emitted a whine. All over a stupid little detention.

Sitting right across from Eva was Breeze, who seemed to be enjoying the girl's torment. A few desks away, Sully tried to get his friend's attention. And he hoped he could do that without getting Ms. Komplin's attention as well.

Each time the teacher turned her back to the class, Sully would wave his arms in Breeze's direction. But the big dummy just kept smiling at Eva.

Sully hissed, "*Ssssst…Breeze.*"

Ms. Komplin swung around. She looked at each fearful face, yet couldn't discern where the sounds had come from. "All of you should be quietly working on the exercises in chapter twelve of your book. Are there any questions about the exercises?"

Silence.

"Good. Then continue." And Ms. Komplin returned to the sentences she was carefully printing on the board.

Sully slid out of his seat. Crawling cautiously but quickly, he moved down the aisle to the back of the classroom, where he traveled past three rows of desks until he came to the row where Breeze was seated. Sully crept up the aisle and surprised his friend.

"*Sul…*" the boy started, but Sully immediately covered his mouth with a hand.

Ms. Komplin spun around again. Sully ducked down as low as he could. The teacher's scowling face once more scanned the classroom. Did she notice the empty desk which Sully had vacated? Apparently not, because she soon resumed her work at the board.

Sully rose a little from his position on the floor. "Stifle that girl," he whispered to his friend.

"Huh?" Breeze didn't seem to know what Sully meant.

"Stifle!" Now Sully punched his fist into his other hand.

Breeze nodded and Sully began to return to his seat, traveling along his previous route. But as he made his way back, the new girl—Vanessa—watched his journey with some amusement. Then as Sully started to crawl up her row, she giggled.

"Someone thinks these exercises are funny?" Ms. Komplin's eyes glistened with delight. "Hmm? Come on now, who's laughing?"

Sully froze along with everyone else. Even the squealer, having learned his lesson from the other day, didn't say a word. But eyes nervously darted about the room. As the new kid in class, Vanessa wasn't yet sure what the others would do. Would they tell on her?

Sully didn't know what to do either. He didn't dare move and risk getting caught. But if Ms. Komplin started walking to her left, she would surely see him there on the floor. Then Vanessa did something unexpected—she stood up right in front of him. Sully crouched lower on the floor.

"I'm sorry, Ms. Komplin," said the girl, "I was thinking of a joke I heard recently and…" She shrugged slightly. "I just had to laugh."

Ms. Komplin moved closer to the aisle in which Vanessa stood. The girl's right hand, now behind her back, motioned for Sully to move backward. He did. And he kept creeping backward until he came to the end of the row. Then he pulled himself behind Bardo, sitting in the last desk. For once, Sully was thankful this guy was so big.

"I always enjoy a good joke," Ms. Komplin was saying. "Please share it with us, Vanessa."

"Um…" the girl hesitated, shuffling her feet a little on the floor.

Does she really have a joke in her head, wondered Sully? He didn't think so. Rising to the occasion, the boy whispered from behind Bardo, "*Why'd the bubblegum cross the road?*"

Vanessa heard and quickly repeated, "Um, do you know why the bubblegum crossed the road?"

"I'll bite," said the teacher with a smile.

"*Cause it was stuck on the chicken's shoe,*" whispered Sully.

"Because it was stuck on the chicken's shoe," repeated the girl.

Ms. Komplin's smile grew bigger. "That's pretty good."

But Sully was just getting started; he had a million chicken jokes. "*Why'd the dinosaur cross the road?*"

"I...have another one," said Vanessa, and she repeated Sully's line.

"*Because there weren't any chickens around yet.*"

Again Vanessa repeated Sully's words, followed by a few groans from her fellow classmates.

But Ms. Komplin seemed amused. And she was still smiling when she said, "All right, that'll do. Let's get started on these sentences on the board."

The teacher moved back to the front of the room; as she did, Sully resumed his travel up the aisle to his desk. Once back in his seat, he swiveled around to look at Vanessa, sitting four desks behind him. He gave her the thumbs up and she smiled sweetly in return. Sully's face suddenly felt warm.

Then WHAM! Breeze had finally done something to stop Eva's whimpering. But now she was all-out crying.

Ms. Komplin immediately came to investigate. "Matthew," she addressed Breeze, "what's going on here?"

The boy donned an innocent look and shook his head. "I dunno, Ms. Komplin. I musta...accidentally...bumped Eva's English book. Guess it fell on her foot."

"You *threw* it there!" screamed Eva.

"Hey, accidents happen," protested Breeze.

As Ms. Komplin tried to sort out what actually took place, Sully kept a lookout for Karmack, who he felt sure was around somewhere.

A small flash in a corner of the classroom—Karmack? Sully kept his eyes on the corner, waiting for another flash. It came a few seconds later, a little to the left of the corner. Then another one, farther from the corner.

Sully stared intently. The flashes were Karmack's movements, no doubt about it. More flashes, one after another, as the creature traveled across the room until it reached where Breeze was standing. *I should warn him. But what good would it do? Karmack's still gonna balance him*. So Sully kept his mouth shut and continued to watch.

Pretty soon Breeze's own English book was rising from his desk and moving fast. WHAM! It slammed down on Breeze's foot.

"Owwww!" the boy cried.

Ms. Komplin couldn't believe what she saw happen. The book seemed to lift on its own and drop onto Breeze's foot. She blinked her eyes a few times and shook her head. "How'd that…?"

Uma snickered. "Karma," she said.

Moments later, Sully's English book also started to levitate, but he didn't see it; his eyes were focused on the other side of the room. Then WHAM! The book dropped on Sully's foot.

"Owwww!" he cried too.

Now Sully was ready to pounce. As soon as Karmack revealed itself, he'd be all over that little guy. And there—some flashes near the classroom door. Sully saw Karmack squeezing through the slightly open door. He took off after the creature.

CHAPTER TEN

The Captive

Sully chased Karmack to the very end of the empty hallway. And just as the creature began to pry open an exit door, the boy grabbed its arm.

"Gotcha again!" said Sully as he held tight to the arm. "You oughta know by now, I always outrun you."

Karmack's face showed despair. "No hurt, no hurt."

Sully glared at the creature. "Begging won't help you this time. I'm taking you back. To show the others who's been causing all the trouble."

Karmack didn't even attempt to struggle. With Sully's tight grip on its arm, the creature walked back to the classroom with the boy.

When they re-entered the room, everyone turned to look. "Oh yeah," Sully said to the class, "betcha ain't seen nothing like this before!"

Yet no one looked shocked. Instead, they seemed… *bewildered?*

"Curtis," said Ms. Komplin, "why'd you bring that tree in here?"

"It's not a tree, it's..." Sully pulled the creature to the front of him. But it wasn't the creature anymore. To Sully's amazement, he was now holding...a baby spruce tree.

"Hey, what happened? Karmack, where are you?" The boy looked around the room, but couldn't find the creature. The little tree was the same size as Karmack, with its roots resting on the floor. Was *this* Karmack?

"Did you just go and pull that thing out of the ground?" Ms. Komplin asked. Sully didn't have an answer for her.

The teacher seemed annoyed. "Stop all these shenanigans, Curtis. Put that tree over by the trash and get back to your seat."

"But Ms. Komplin...this isn't really a tree." Sully looked very serious. Yet most of the students were staring wide-eyed at the boy. "Tell them, Karmack. Tell them it's you."

The tree didn't utter a sound.

"Why won't you talk? Tell them, or I'll clobber you."

Even that failed to get a response.

Sully decided to pinch one of its branches, just to make the creature cry out. But before he could, Ms. Komplin had the boy by the earlobe and was dragging him back to his desk. "I *said*... that's enough of this nonsense."

She was hurting Sully's ear, yet the boy refused to let go of the tree. So Karmack dragged along behind Sully to his desk. Tired of arguing, Ms. Komplin let Sully place the tree in the aisle next to his desk until recess, when he would have to dispose of it outside.

As the teacher resumed their English lesson, Sully whispered to Karmack, "You ain't getting away again. Ever!"

Ms. Komplin completed the lesson, and the bell for recess rang. Students jumped from their seats and sped for the door. But not Sully and Karmack. The boy was still holding tight to the tree.

"Hey Sul, you coming?" called Gonzo at the door.

"You go ahead. I'll catch up."

"Suit yourself," said Gonzo as he and Breeze departed, leaving Sully alone with the tree. Ms. Komplin had left to run an errand.

"Why'd you change into a tree?" he demanded.

The creature instantly resumed its normal appearance. "I's no can show."

"But you show yourself to *me*."

"You's only see because speedy-eyed. You's see before I's can change."

Sully sighed. "So I can't show you to anybody."

"No show."

The boy slammed a book down on his desk; Karmack jumped a little. "Look, I don't wanna hurt you, but you gotta stop all this balancing."

"But I's job…"

"Forget the stupid job. Leave me alone. Just leave us *all* alone."

Karmack furrowed its tiny brow and frowned. "No can. This mean…I's be hurt? You's…hurt?"

The boy looked to the side. "Don't know…what else I can do. Can't just…let you keep balancing me. And I can't do all that goody-goody stuff neither."

"You's do today. With girl."

"Huh?"

"Girl. You's give jokes. She's be happy. Good trick."

"You mean Vanessa? She's okay, I guess. For a girl."

"You's balance one bad trick with good trick. One less I's need balance."

Sully hadn't thought of that. "Yeah but, there's still a skyscraper up there, right?'

"'Xactly."

"But I can't do lots of good tricks. So you'll still be dumping on me."

"Why you's no can do?"

"Like I told you, Karmack, I got a reputation to uphold. I'm the number one guy in this school. And being tough is what keeps me number one. If I turn into Mr. Nice Guy, kids won't respect me anymore. And I'll stop being the Big Cheese."

Karmack looked confused. "You's do bad tricks so be… happy?"

"That's right. I'm prob'ly not like any of those other slobs you've balanced in the past. Doing bad tricks makes me happy. So…you gonna leave me alone now?"

Karmack shuffled its little bare feet as Sully continued to grip its arm. The creature's head dropped when it finally responded, "You's be I's job."

That did it. Sully pulled the little guy closer and grabbed it around the waist. Then he lifted Karmack and carried it out of the room, passing kids in the hallway who had no idea why Sully was holding that baby tree out in front of him. Karmack, of course, kept quiet.

Sully took the creature into the gym, where he knew he'd find some rope in the equipment room. Then, while holding on to Karmack with one hand, he quickly looped the rope around the creature's midsection and tied a strong knot in back.

"Put your hand back here," he told the creature.

Karmack tried to reach its backside, but couldn't.

"Just as I thought," said Sully. "Those pudgy little arms are too short to get at my knot." Then he dragged Karmack by the rope, out of the school, through the yard, and to the woods behind. Of course, kids in the schoolyard only saw Sully dragging a little tree.

The two stopped at a small clearing. Sully then looped the free end of the rope around a maple tree, bringing it to tie with the knot on Karmack's back. Once the rope was secure and Sully felt confident the creature couldn't reach the knot, he sat down next to the tree.

"You got about fifteen feet," he told Karmack, "to move around the clearing."

"I's prisoner," said the sad face with the big nose.

"Got that right. Now I can be me again, not having to worry about your stupid balancing."

"But I's job..."

"Think of it this way: I'm putting you on vacation. Until school's out for the summer. Then I'll set you free. Hey, what do you eat anyway?"

"I's eat forest food."

"Can you reach any of it from here?"

Karmack looked around the clearing. "I's can reach."

"Good. Do you...drink water?"

"I's drink from stream."

"There's no stream in these woods. I'll have to bring you water from home. Can you drink from a bottle?"

"I's drink from stream."

Sully thought about that. "How about a dog bowl? Could you manage that?" He cupped his hands to approximate the size of the bowl.

"Dog bowl...okay."

Sully nodded. "I know you're not gonna enjoy being tied up, Karmack, but at least I'm not clobbering you. Don't worry, I'll check on you every day, make sure you're okay. You'll be like...my secret pet."

Karmack seemed about to cry. "But...I's no balance...you's boys—dreadful, awful doom!"

"You let *me* worry about that." Then Sully took off for the schoolyard.

As Karmack watched him go, there was anguish on its little face. "Dreadful, awful doom. Dreadful awful."

CHAPTER ELEVEN
Change in Behavior

Sully did in fact worry about the doom Karmack predicted. And how that skyscraper might still fall on his head. He thought maybe if he were a bit more careful and avoided doing so *many* bad tricks, he might keep it from toppling. At least until he released Karmack in the summer, when the creature could resume its balancing.

But there were still six weeks of fifth grade left. Could Sully manage to control his impulses that long? And what about Karmack? He didn't want to get the little guy in trouble. What if the universe needed the creature to generate a hurricane, or even a tsunami? Could some other nature spirit do it instead?

These were the worries that kept Sully awake most of the night following his abduction of the creature. And even when he finally drifted off, Sully soon woke screaming. In his nightmare, herds of little Karmacks were carting him off to be eaten.

The following morning, Sully remembered to check on the little guy before school. Karmack seemed to be doing just fine. So Sully left the dog bowl, placing some bottled water beside it.

He showed Karmack how to open the bottles and pour the water into the bowl. As soon as Sully finished demonstrating, the thirsty creature dove for the bowl and started lapping the water like a dog. The boy howled with laughter.

Minutes later, entering his classroom, Sully saw Ms. Komplin staring down at something in the left-hand drawer of her desk. A small tear also trickled down the woman's cheek. But when Ms. Komplin caught the boy watching her, she slammed the drawer shut.

"All right, class," Ms. Komplin said as she clapped her hands together. "The first order of business is a new seating plan."

Everyone groaned. This was a major operation, requiring all students to transfer their desks to a different row. One hour later, when the dust had settled, Sully found himself in his row's second seat with one girl in front and another behind him. Breeze and Gonzo, now closer to the back of the room, seemed miles away.

Yet Sully considered himself lucky. Ms. Komplin had put Vanessa to the front of him. She was nice. Behind him was Abigail, and she'd no doubt kick Sully when she had the chance. But Breeze and Gonzo weren't so lucky, with mean girls both in front and in back of them.

Until now, Sully thought of girls only as creatures he liked to torment. With worms, caterpillars, snakes—anything that made them shriek or say, "Ewwww, yucky!" But Vanessa…well, she was different. Sully wasn't thinking of tormenting her. She was pretty. Real pretty, with big brown eyes and long straight hair falling down her back. Pretty. Real pretty. And nice. She smiled when he looked at her. And that made his face feel warm.

The other girls had warned Vanessa about Sully and his gang. But because she hadn't already spent four years experiencing their torment, Vanessa wasn't put off by these boys. She actually found Sully's behavior kind of interesting. And she thought he was cute, too.

By midmorning, Sully was starting to feel the effects of not getting enough sleep. Ms. Komplin was in the middle of a history lesson, droning on about the Civil War battle of Gettysburg. Since the battle site was located in their own state of Pennsylvania, the entire fifth grade was scheduled for a three-day field trip there at the end of term. Everyone was looking forward to that.

But prior to the Gettysburg trip, the fifth graders would be treated to a one-day visit to the town of Blairsville, just an hour's drive from the school. There they would learn about the town's connection with the Underground Railroad, that secret pre-Civil War network which assisted slaves making their way north to freedom. The day would include a reenactment of Blairsville's famous Rescue of 1848, when the townspeople mobbed bounty hunters seeking a fugitive slave who'd been living there for six years as a free man.

Sully was excited about the upcoming trips. He really liked history, especially anything having to do with the Civil War. But on this day, he couldn't keep his mind focused on the history lesson. His eyelids were fluttering and he could feel his head getting heavy. Before he knew it, his head had suddenly dropped, which caused him to snap it right back up. When this happened a second time, Sully realized he'd better give in to a quick nap. He placed his head over folded arms on top of his open history book.

Ms. Komplin was narrating the story of the famous Pickett's Charge at Gettysburg. As Vanessa listened to the story, she began to hear a sound in the background. It was coming from behind her, and sounded like a bear: *Grrnzzzzz*. She spun around to find Sully snoring.

Reaching over the back of her seat, Vanessa poked at Sully's arm. "Wake up," the girl whispered.

But Sully didn't rouse. So Vanessa poked harder and spoke louder. "Wake up!"

That worked. Sully's eyes blinked as he lifted his head. But Ms. Komplin had also heard something and looked over as Vanessa was saying, "Boy, that was a close one."

The teacher paused in her narration and marched straight to the board. Then in the top right hand corner, she wrote Vanessa's name on the detention list.

Sully saw the girl's shoulders droop. He felt dreadful. Vanessa had got in trouble for trying to keep *him* out of trouble.

He raced to the front of the room. "Ms. Komplin, Vanessa only said one word. *One word!*" Of course she'd said more than one word, but this was a tiny lie compared to the whoppers he'd told in the past. "And it was *my* fault. Don't punish *her,* punish me."

The teacher couldn't believe those words came from Curtis Sullenburg's mouth. Sully could hardly believe it himself. He was defending a...*girl?* What was happening to him?

Students watched, their mouths open, as Sully continued to implore Ms. Komplin to take Vanessa's name off the detention list. No one had ever seen Sully behave this way. And Breeze and Gonzo, already worried about their leader's mental state, became alarmed.

Vanessa, however, was absolutely delighted—just like a fairytale princess, she had a brave knight coming to her rescue. Could any girl ask for more?

Ms. Komplin warned Sully that if he didn't stop begging, he'd get detention as well. So of course, Sully continued to beg. Then he walked back to his seat smiling, as the teacher wrote his name beneath Vanessa's. Though Sully didn't know what his detention might be, for the moment at least, he felt victorious.

After school, those students with detention (there were four) met with Ms. Komplin. She handed out assignments for each. Winston and Jake were told to help Mr. Sorenson, the janitor, give all the dry-erase boards in the school a thorough washing. Vanessa was to help Ms. Komplin correct homework papers, and Sully was sent to the principal's office because this was his tenth detention in a month. So, instead of spending time after school with Vanessa, Sully had to endure a lecture from Principal Devers.

He survived the lecture by half-listening while considering what his next move might be. Sully needed to get someone to believe him. About Karmack. Because the whole business was starting to drive the boy crazy.

That evening, he called Gonzo and Breeze at their homes. He told them to meet him early the next morning because he had something special to show them.

CHAPTER TWELVE

Skyscraper on the Precipice

Sully arrived in the schoolyard before his friends. In his backpack were six more bottles for Karmack. His mother had expressed surprise at all the water Sully had been drinking lately, but she was in favor of this and started to buy extra bottles.

When Breeze and Gonzo showed up, Sully led them into the woods. At the clearing, the boys saw the rope Sully had looped around the maple tree. They also saw the opposite end of the rope knotted into a smaller loop which was moving around and around the tree, causing sparks of light as it went by them. But Breeze and Gonzo couldn't see anything inside the loop.

"H…how you doing that?" Gonzo asked.

"That's my prisoner," replied Sully. Both boys stared at him. "I know you can't see the little dude. Nobody can, except for me. But he's here, inside that rope."

Sully went to the rope and yanked on it to get Karmack to stop. "C'mon, Karmack, cool it." But the creature refused. It just kept flying back and forth around the tree at top speed. Sully tried to grab the creature as it whizzed by, but he couldn't. Finally, he tugged on the rope, pulling the creature slowly toward him. As he did, Karmack transformed once again into the baby spruce tree.

"Hey, that's some magic trick!" admired Breeze.

"I'm holding…the creature," Sully said, lifting it off the ground. Although small, Karmack was heavy. "C'mon over… and touch it."

"Touch the tree?" said Gonzo.

"It's not really a tree, it just looks like one. It's really like…a gnome. You know, like the gnomes in fairytales."

Breeze and Gonzo didn't know what to make of all this. Gonzo stuck out his hand to touch the tree, not expecting to feel anything other than spruce needles.

Yet Karmack wasn't about to let itself be touched. Summoning a power it kept in reserve, the creature forced itself out of Sully's hands and raced away from the boys.

"Huh? How'd you do *that?*" Breeze asked as he watched the rope move to the other side of the tree.

"Oh man, Sully," said Gonzo. "I dunno *how* you're doing this, but it's…*excellent.* You been learning magic tricks from some famous magician?"

But Sully wasn't listening. He was chasing after Karmack again. The creature kept eluding his grasp, racing full speed around the tree and back. Breeze and Gonzo stood there watching, their mouths wide open. They couldn't imagine how Sully was making this rope move in such an erratic pattern.

Eventually Sully was able to grab hold of the rope and once more reel Karmack back to him. Then he sat on the creature, which resembled a tree again. "Owwww," it shouted in a squeaky little voice.

"Who said that?" Gonzo wanted to know.

"The creature," said Sully. "Name's Karmack." Then he started to pinch the little tree, hard. "Owwww. No hurt, no hurt!"

Breeze took a step backward. So did Gonzo. "Man, Sully, you some kind of vent…ventril…you know, one of them guys who talks through a dummy?'

"Nah, it's really the creature talking. C'mere and touch."

Now Breeze moved forward, extending his hand as far as the rope. Gonzo moved forward as well. Their fingers gingerly touched at the spruce needles, but what they felt was soft and spongy like…an arm. Breeze moved farther down the arm and felt…little fingers!

"Aiiiiiiiii," screamed the boy, fear flashing in his eyes. "That tree's…a ghost!" Breeze took off, followed by Gonzo.

Sully rolled off Karmack. "Geeze, I got wimps for a gang!"

The creature stood and brushed the dirt off its tunic. "You's no nice. I's be hurt."

"Only trying to get a sound outta ya. If you'd cooperated, I wouldn't have hurt you." Sully then remembered the bottles in his backpack; he dumped them next to the water bowl.

Karmack looked above the boy's head. "You's do better. I's can see."

"Huh? Whattaya see?"

"You's help girl. Two times. She's be happy."

"Oh, that. Yeah, I just thought her being new and all…" Sully felt his face getting warm again.

"One less trick I's need balance."

"One less, huh? Tell me something, Karmack—you gotta balance *all* the bad tricks I've ever done, in my whole entire life?"

"All bad tricks need balance. If you's no balance, be I's job."

"Lemme make sure I got this right. Every bad trick I ever did *has* to be balanced?"

"All need balance. You's can do, or I's do."

"So that means you'll be hounding me for the rest of my life?"

"No hound. Balance. One side scale balance other."

Sully kicked his heel into the hard ground. "That don't seem right."

"You's friend, I's see new bad trick over head. Skyscraper fall soon."

"Huh? Whattayamean?!"

"Boy who here. Skyscraper fall soon."

"For certain?"

Karmack nodded vigorously.

"Which one? Gonzo or Breeze?"

The creature didn't seem to understand the question.

"Which one? Breeze, the tall one?" Sully held a flat palm about a foot over his head; Breeze was very tall for his age. "Or the shorter one—with the unibrow?" Sully now lowered his palm to approximate Gonzo's height and ran his finger across his eyebrows.

When Karmack continued to stare, Sully positioned both hands at the height of each boy. "Which one, tall or short?"

So the creature did the same, placing one hand higher than the other. Then Karmack smiled and began moving the hands up and down like it was directing a symphony orchestra.

"You have no idea what I'm talking about, do you?"

"Gotcha!"

In the distance, Sully could hear the school bell ringing. He had to run. "Gimme a clue here. Which boy has a skyscraper about to fall?"

Yet Karmack still didn't seem to understand. "Boy you's friend."

Sully gave up and headed out of the woods. Now he had an even bigger worry. One of his friends was about to face a dreadful, awful doom. But which one? And was there anything he could do to stop it?

CHAPTER THIRTEEN

Doom for Whom?

As Sully walked toward his school, all he could think about was Justin Berley, the Abominable Snowman of pigeon poop. Would that be Gonzo's doom? Breeze's, maybe? Which boy would get pooped on? Whose skyscraper would topple? Or could Sully stop it from happening?

Entering the classroom, he saw that Ms. Komplin hadn't yet arrived. Sully looked to the back of the room to find his friends. And there was Gonzo, red in the face and about to smack another guy in the kisser.

Sully raced to stop him. Grabbing Gonzo's clenched fist, he ordered, "Hold it."

Gonzo seemed stunned. "Why you telling me to hold it? This guy needs to get pounded." The intended victim ducked out of the way and ran to the other side of the room.

"Let him go," said Sully.

Gonzo's face turned even redder. "What's gotten into you, Sul? I don't even know you anymore."

"Trust me on this. No good woulda come from pounding that kid."

Gonzo was still mad. "You should *never* get in the way of a pounding…"

Then Sully noticed Breeze a few feet away, holding Sophia's lunch bag high in the air. For as long as Sully could remember, Breeze had a habit of rummaging through other kids's lunches. He assumed the boy was always hungry because he had such a long body to fill.

Sully turned to Breeze and asked, "What you planning to do with that?"

"Just gonna see if there's anything I'd like for lunch today," he answered with a laugh. Sophia, meanwhile, was desperately grabbing at her bag. Towering over the girl, Breeze tipped the bag and looked inside while keeping it out of her reach. "Hmmm. Looks like a homemade brownie. Think I'll have that."

Sophia yelled, "Gimme my bag, gimme my bag."

But as Breeze reached inside for the brownie, Sully jumped onto a desk and snatched the bag away from him.

"Hey, whatcha doing, Sul?"

"Saving you," he replied, handing Sophia her lunch.

"Saving me from what? Brownie poisoning?"

"Trust me, okay? You don't wanna take that lunch."

"Why not?"

Sully had to think fast. And what he recollected was that Breeze hated—*absolutely loathed*—being sick, even if it were just a head cold. Motioning Breeze to bend lower, Sully whispered in the boy's ear, "Sophia's whole family just got over the flu."

Breeze looked as if he were about to faint. "They *did?*"

"Yeah. Haven't you noticed how pale she looks?"

Of course, Sully had no idea whether Sophia's family had succumbed to the flu. But he knew Breeze wouldn't go anywhere near the girl's lunch now.

But what Sully failed to realize was that this excuse wouldn't stop Breeze from trying to grab *other* lunch bags. "How about Melanie? Her family get the flu?"

He had to think fast again. "No…not yet. But look how close Mel's desk is to Sophia's."

"Oh, yeah. Guess that's not a good idea. I should try girls on the other side of the room." As Breeze started to walk away, Sully followed. He was wondering how long he'd have to keep this up—making sure his friends stayed out of trouble.

Ms. Komplin then entered the classroom, saving Sully from having to find another excuse to stop Breeze. The teacher called the class to order and made the regular morning announcements. Then she began to explain how the class would be preparing for their upcoming trip to Gettysburg National Military Park.

"Each fifth grade class has been assigned a different project for the trip. Our theme is 'Life of the Civil War Soldier.' Each of you will assume the identity of a real man who actually fought at the battle of Gettysburg. You will proudly display this man's name and military rank on your ID badges. Then you will learn actual drill commands and practice marching like the soldiers did at Gettysburg. We will also design and create a class flag to take with us that day. And finally…we'll make the food that men ate on the battlefield. Each of you will be including this food in your field trip lunches."

Molly asked how they would choose the names of their soldiers.

"I have a list," replied Ms. Komplin. "We'll hold a class election for the six officers of the company, and those of you who aren't chosen will take the names of privates on the list."

The election of officers yielded the expected result—Sully was chosen the company's captain. As Higgins's Big Cheese, he wouldn't have accepted anything less.

The officers were instructed to make insignia patches, denoting their ranks, to wear on their sleeves or shoulders. Sully and the other elected officers went to the side table to copy the samples Ms. Komplin placed there. The rest of the students engaged in a brainstorming session for the design of their class flag. Once they agreed on the general theme, Ms. Komplin told them to individually sketch a design. Later, everyone would vote on which was best.

As Sully worked on his captain's bars, he kept glancing back at the class, hoping his friends weren't getting into any trouble. It was a good thing he did. Because while the students were sketching, Ms. Komplin's attention was once more diverted by something in her desk drawer.

Sully saw Gonzo whisper to Breeze. *What're those knuckleheads up to?* Then Gonzo began to move quietly along the back wall of the room until he reached Allison Waters's desk. Here was a girl who had artistic talent and everyone knew it; she even kept a full bundle of colored pencils in her desk for occasions such as this.

Breeze was snickering as he watched Gonzo creep up behind Allison. That's when Sully spied the packet of ketchup Gonzo was holding at his back. Now he knew what the boy was up to. But could he get there before Gonzo squirted ketchup all over Allison's sketch?

A tear was once again sliding down Ms. Komplin's cheek. Only when she heard the thump did she look up. And there was Gonzo, sprawled in the aisle next to Allison's desk. Sully was lying on top of him.

Ms. Komplin immediately rose to address the boys. "What's going on back there?"

"I…um, tripped," explained Sully while lifting himself off his friend. "Then I bumped into Gonz…I mean, Carlos."

"Yeah," said Gonzo, as he rose from the floor, ketchup splattered all over his face.

Ms. Komplin raced over. "Are you hurt?"

"No, I just fell."

"But the blood…?"

"What blood?" That's when Gonzo realized his face felt kind of moist. He reached up and dabbed at the ketchup. "Oh, this! I musta busted the ketchup packet when I fell."

Everyone began to laugh. Except Ms. Komplin. "Why were you holding the ketchup in the first place?"

But then the bell for recess rang, saving Gonzo from having to fabricate a believable lie. Sully breathed a sigh of relief. So far, he'd been able to forestall disaster.

Yet if Karmack was right, it was still just a matter of time.

CHAPTER FOURTEEN

All Fall Down

When spring ushered in warmer temperatures in Western Pennsylvania, the fifth grade girls resumed their jump-rope games at recess. A girl at each end would turn a long rope as a third girl jumped between them. And just like their mothers, grandmothers, and even great-grandmothers before them, these girls repeated rhymes as they jumped.

On this particular day, blessed with blue skies and a smiling sun, one girl jumped as the others chanted, "Scrambled eggs, butter on toast. Who's the boy you like the most? First name, A…B…C…" and so on until the girl jumped out of the rope at the initial of the boy's first name. Then she would return to do the same for the initial of the boy's last name. The others would have to guess from the initials which boy the girl liked.

"C'mon, Vanessa, you're next," shouted Abigail, holding one end of the rope.

"Think I'll pass," replied Vanessa. "I hardly know any boys yet."

"You know the ones in our class."

"Yeah, but…oh, all right."

Down at the other end of the schoolyard, Sully was trying to convince his two friends to return to the woods with him. He was hoping Karmack would finger the one whose skyscraper was about to topple, because it was proving too much for him to keep an eye on them both.

"It's not a magic trick…or a ghost," Sully was saying. "There really is someone there. A nature spirit. And he's flesh and blood like us. Only he won't let you see him. That's why he turns into a tree when I catch him."

Gonzo squinted at Sully. "So's how come *you* can see him?"

"Karmack said it's because I got speedy eyes. And most people don't."

Breeze gave a snort. "Yeah, right!"

"Sul, you're going mental on us," Gonzo said. "And I want no part of it." The boy dismissed the matter with a wave and began to walk away.

"No, wait! Just come with me, one last time. Okay? Hey… I'll, um…give you each ten bucks. All right?"

Gonzo was skeptical. "You *got* ten bucks? For each of us?"

Sully shuffled his feet. "No…but I'll get it. Soon. Trust me."

But still Gonzo didn't want to go. He shook his head.

"What about you, Breeze? You wanna earn an easy ten dollars?"

He did. "Yeah, okay. Just one last time. But I'm not going near the ghost."

That was good enough. Sully just needed Karmack to tell him if this boy was the one with the skyscraper about to fall.

Breeze followed Sully to the woods. But just as they were about to enter, one of the gang's wannabes ran up to Sully. "You…won't…believe it," Stefan panted.

"Believe what?" Sully asked.

"Vanessa…she's got…a crush on you!"

Sully could feel his face warming again. "Vanessa?"

"Yeah, man! She just spelled out…your initials…at the jumping rope. I heard it." Some of the boys liked to hang around as the girls jumped, especially when they were playing this particular game.

"You sure she meant *me?*"

"Yeah, man! None of the girls could figure out who C. S. was. So Vanessa said your name. First girl who ever liked you, huh?"

That made the Big Cheese's face get hotter. "Whattayamean? Lots of girls like me."

Stefan took a step backward and raised a hand in surrender. "Just joking, Sul. 'Course they like you. They *all* like you."

Sully turned his head in the direction of the girls who were jumping rope. He could see Vanessa watching from the sidelines. Was this *true*, he wondered? Did she really like him?

Breeze started to laugh. "Man, some stupid girl likes you! Who cares? Ain't that right, Sully?"

The Big Cheese glared at him. *He* cared. It was Vanessa. And she wasn't stupid.

"Hey, we going in the woods or not?" Breeze asked.

"In a minute. You wait here." Sully moved briskly in the direction of the rope jumpers. Stefan was at his heels, trying to keep up. When they reached the girls, Sully stopped. Stefan, not expecting him to stop so abruptly, bumped into the boy's backside.

Two girls giggled. They pointed at Sully, and Vanessa turned to see. She smiled at him, like always.

For the first time in his life, Sully didn't know what to say. He just stared at Vanessa. Then he got an idea. He motioned for her to step away from the rope jumpers.

Once the two were alone, Sully asked her, "You, ah…wanna sit with me? I mean, on the field trip bus, to Blairsville?"

The girl's eyes lit up. "Sure, okay."

"All right, then." Sully looked down at his feet. What else could he say to her?

"Yeah, all right," said Vanessa.

Maybe he'd give her a little compliment. "I, uh, like that… clip, in your hair."

"Yeah, really?"

"Sure. It's nice."

"Well, what *you* did the other day…that was nice too. I mean, when Ms. Komplin gave me detention for talking to you."

Sully shrugged. "It was nothing."

"No, it was really…nice."

The boy looked up and saw the girl smiling again. He smiled back.

Then out of nowhere, he felt someone smack him from behind. It was Bardo. Gonzo had pushed the boy, and he'd fallen backward into Sully.

Man, these guys just can't stay outta trouble. Sully spun around and screamed, "Cool it, you guys. Cool it *now.*"

Both boys froze. Sully's glare was so icy, his face so furious, they didn't dare move. "You punks gotta stop all this fighting." Then he shouted at them, "Go on, get outta here."

Though somewhat stunned, Gonzo and Bardo did as they were ordered by the Big Cheese.

When Sully turned back to Vanessa, he saw that she had rejoined her jumping group. But she was still watching him. And smiling. Then Sully remembered—he'd left Breeze at the edge of the woods. He gave Vanessa a slight wave and took off.

But Breeze was no longer at the woods. *Where'd he go?*

It was too late to find out. The bell was ringing, signaling the end of recess.

* * * *

When lunchtime came, Sully made sure to follow behind Breeze in the cafeteria line. Gonzo was toting a bag lunch since he didn't care for the day's menu selections. But Sully was mostly concerned about Breeze, since the boy usually found a way to sneak already-purchased food from the trays of unsuspecting kids. Sully knew he couldn't let that happen, not with a skyscraper ready to topple.

As the students inched along the cafeteria line, the two girls in front of Breeze were so busy chatting they were slowing the line for everyone behind them. "Hey, keep it moving," Sully shouted. The girls turned to stare; then picked up their pace a little.

Sully could see Gonzo take a seat at their regular table. Three of the wannabes were there too. He saw them talking together. Then Gonzo reached over to grab one of them. Sully's blood pressure began to skyrocket. *Leave him alone, Gonz. Just leave the kid alone.*

But Gonzo wouldn't. Both of his hands grasped Stefan's collar. There was no time to lose—Gonzo was about to punch that kid.

Sully abandoned his food tray on the line and raced for the table. And he got there just in time to stop Gonzo from…*wait a minute!* These guys were all smiling.

"Whatsamatter, Sul?" asked Gonzo.

"What…you doing with Stefan's shirt?"

Gonzo laughed. "Just showing him what happened last night on *American Gangsters*." That was a TV show about crime syndicates in 1930s Chicago; all the boys watched it.

"Missed it last night," said Stefan.

For once, Gonzo wasn't being aggressive—who would've guessed?

Sully snarled at them and headed back to the cafeteria line. Breeze was leaving the cashier with his tray of food. But right next to him, those two girls were still engrossed in conversation; they didn't see Breeze lift a pudding cup from one of their trays.

Sully had to stop this; he had to convince Breeze to put it back. He picked up his pace.

But just as Breeze was about to make his getaway, he tripped. His food tray went flying. And as he fell, Breeze's head hit the steel counter of the cafeteria line, smacking his jaw into it. By the time the boy landed on the floor, blood was spurting from his mouth, along with several teeth.

Oh man! Sully couldn't believe this was happening. Breeze's skyscraper had toppled before he had a chance to do anything about it.

The principal arrived minutes later to assess the situation. He ordered the cafeteria supervisor to call for an ambulance right away. Sully and Gonzo stayed by their friend's side until the ambulance arrived.

"You'll be okay, man," Sully assured him.

"Yeah," Gonzo said, "the doctors can probably sew your teeth back in."

Sew his teeth back in? This dude's dumb as a stump.

But Breeze wouldn't be okay. They found out the next day that the boy's jaw had been broken. Doctors at the hospital wired it together. It would take months to heal, and Breeze would be eating through a straw during that time.

Man, a liquid diet.

Now Sully was really worried. What if his own skyscraper toppled before he could balance it? He couldn't begin to imagine what dreadful, awful doom might lie ahead.

CHAPTER FIFTEEN

Growing Up

The following Saturday, Sully took more bottled water to the woods behind the school. But when he reached the clearing, he didn't see Karmack. The maple tree was there, *yet where was the rope?*

Sully ran around the tree, looking for signs of life. Then a shrill cry came from above as Karmack plopped onto his head. The creature had climbed the tree and pulled the rope up too.

"Gotcha," shrieked Karmack as Sully tried to dislodge the creature from his head. But its fingers clutched stubbornly at the boy's hair.

"Get off, get off," Sully shouted.

The creature climbed down him, laughing all the while.

"What's the big idea?" asked Sully.

"I's gotcha!"

"Yeah, you got me all right. Very funny." But Sully wasn't at all amused.

Once on the ground, Karmack wobbled a bit and tried to steady its legs.

"What's the matter? You sleepy or something?"

"I's…*hic.*"

"You're what?"

The creature hiccuped again and wobbled to its left.

Sully shouted, "You're drunk."

"I's…*hic*…drink water. From…*hic*…bottle you's bring."

The boy went over to the dog bowl. He put a finger in the clear liquid there and tasted it. "Awgh! This ain't water!" Sully looked around. "Where's the bottle this came from?"

A search of the area revealed some empty bottles under a bush. "Spring water, spring water," Sully said, as he smelled each one. "Wait! This one's not spring water—it's vodka!"

Karmack teetered again before dropping down next to the boy. "Taste…bad. Be funny water." Then the creature roared with laughter.

"You *are* drunk," said Sully. "I know vodka's plenty potent. I better stay with you awhile, make sure you don't hurt yourself."

Sully removed the water bottles from his pack, checking their labels carefully. Then he dumped the remaining liquid from the dog bowl and replaced it with fresh water. He sat down on his usual log. "Sorry that happened, Karmack—my bringing the liquor by mistake. My mom sometimes pours vodka in empty water bottles so my dad won't drink too much. But she makes a little mark on the label. A little "v". She musta forgot to do that this time."

"Be…*hic*…bad trick, for you's mom."

"No, it was just a mistake. You know, like an accident."

"Ahhhh, accy-dent!" Karmack plopped down next to him on the log. "I's gotcha." With its eyes half closed, the creature grinned the silliest grin Sully had ever seen. "Accy-dents…*hic*… happen."

"That's right. I think you're finally getting it."

Karmack winked at him. "I's gotcha."

The boy picked up a stick and started pitching it into the dirt. Karmack's chin dropped to its chest. Pretty soon, Sully heard some snoring. "Yeah, sleep it off, little dude," the boy said, mostly to himself.

While the creature slept, Sully thought about what had happened to Breeze. Would something similar befall him and Gonzo? He continued to pitch the stick.

About twenty minutes went by before Karmack began to stir. Then it shook its little head fiercely; Sully had to lean away to keep from getting struck. "You okay now?" he asked.

The creature nodded. "I's drink; then be better." Karmack rose and went to the water bowl, walking a bit more steadily now. After a few laps of water, the creature returned to the log. "You's be sad?"

"Yeah, how'd you know?"

"Can feel you's."

Sully grimaced. "Well, it's Breeze. He got hurt the other day. Broke his jaw."

"Boy's skyscraper fall?"

"Yeah."

"I's see coming," Karmack reminded him.

"Y'know," said Sully, as his stick stabbed at the ground, "I really tried to protect Breeze, tried to keep him safe."

"You's no can. Only I's can, or boy."

Sully pitched the stick harder into the ground. "That ain't right. I knew about the skyscraper and shoulda been able to help."

Karmack looked above the boy's head. "You's try help. I's can see. You's balance more bad tricks."

"Great! The only thing I did was help myself. Couldn't even save my friend." He slammed the stick into the dirt. "What good is it…being speedy-eyed…if all I see is *you?*"

Karmack seemed to understand. "I's can save you's other friend. If…I's be free."

Sully looked closely at the creature. "Tell you what. I promise to set you free if you show yourself to my friends. Not as a tree, but the way I see you. You do that, and I'll untie the rope."

The creature's face fell. "No can do. I's can no let humans see. Forbidden. No can do."

"But you let *me* see you. And talk with you, too."

"Can no stop, on accounta you's…"

"I know—speedy-eyed. Tell me something, Karmack. When does all this balancing end? I mean, if I weren't speedy-eyed and couldn't see you, how would I know I needed to be balanced? I'd just keep pulling pranks, and you'd keep clobbering me…and this would go on and on…like, *forever?*"

"No. You's boy. Still be learning. After much balance, you's stop bad tricks."

"So you're saying—after being clobbered over and over again, I'd be so tired of it I'd… just stop pranking?"

" 'Xactly! You's be learning."

"Well, you sure teach a tough lesson."

"Be I's job."

The two were quiet for a while, as Sully continued to pitch the stick. Then the boy sighed. "I give up." He reached over and began to untie the knot at Karmack's back.

"I's be free?"

"So you can do your job again. I'm no good at it."

As soon as the creature was free of the rope, it began to dance, arms and legs flailing in every direction. It was the funniest dance Sully had ever seen.

The boy then removed the loop from around the maple tree and began winding the rope around his arm.

Karmack sang out, "I's be free! I's be freeeeeeee!"

"You're free all right," said Sully as he turned to leave. "Now be sure and save Gonzo from his skyscraper, okay? I don't wanna see another friend end up like Breeze."

"I's do," said the creature as it continued to dance, "very much good job. I's save you's and you's friend!"

"Forget about me. I don't need saving anymore. My days of pranking are over."

Karmack stopped dancing. "You's stop bad tricks?"

"They're just no fun anymore."

The creature snapped its fingers with excitement. "Ah, you's growing up."

"Growing up, huh? Yeah well, that's not much fun either."

Karmack winked at him. "Fun change now. You's find new fun."

"New fun?"

"I's see." Karmack was pointing above the boy's head. "New fun. With girl."

Sully's face got that warm feeling again. It was doing that a lot lately.

"But…" pondered Karmack, "you's no more need respect? For be Big Cheese?"

"Thought I did. Don't know anymore. Breeze's getting hurt, it changed things."

The creature nodded. "You's be okay now. I's see."

Sully wasn't so sure. "But what about my skyscraper, Karmack? What if I…happen to do something—y'know, outta habit—that adds to the pile? Will it still fall over?"

"Could fall. But shortcut be open now."

"Shortcut? What shortcut?"

"Way for skyscraper go *poof!* Now you's growing up, shortcut open."

"I can get rid of my skyscraper…by taking a shortcut?"

"Pile go *poof* if you's take shortcut."

"But what *is* the shortcut?"

"I's no can tell. You's must find."

"Great," said the boy as he kicked at the dirt. "There's a shortcut that'll get rid of my skyscraper, but you won't tell me what it is."

"No can!" The creature looked genuinely sorry. "I's no can!"

This wasn't what Sully wanted to hear. How could he find the shortcut if he didn't even know what it was?

But he would soon enough.

CHAPTER SIXTEEN

Whiff of Doom

For the next few days, Sully kept himself in line. No teasing, no pranking, no punching. He didn't even threaten guys.

Yet every time Sully turned around, it seemed Gonzo was being balanced by Karmack. Just the day before, when the boys passed a little girl on the street, Gonzo had stuck his chewing gum in her hair; he thought this was funny. Sully just rolled his eyes. Later when Gonzo got home, he saw workers plastering a wall in his house. And wouldn't you know, he immediately tripped over *something*, falling head first into a bucket of plaster. His mother had quite a time getting all that plaster out of the boy's hair—in some spots, she even had to cut it.

"Gonz," Sully said to him the next day at school, "ain't you noticed how all this bad stuff keeps happening to you? Right after you pull a prank?"

"Huh?"

"You know, like the plaster getting stuck in your hair, right after you put that gum in the girl's hair. Don't it seem that fate keeps smacking you in the butt?"

Gonzo scratched his head, pulling at the small bits of hair his mother had cut the day before. "I don't know what you're talking about, Sul."

"Well, think about it. Next time you pull a prank, watch what happens. See if something like it don't boomerang back to you." Breeze had returned to school by now, and his ears perked up when Sully used him to illustrate his point. "Remember what happened to Breeze here? That could happen to you, Gonz. He stole so many lunches, and now look at him—he can't open his mouth to eat!"

It was true. Breeze could barely even speak with his jaws wired shut. His lunch came packed with a straw. But at least he wasn't stealing food from other kids' lunches and trays anymore.

"So watch what happens," Sully repeated.

Gonzo just kept scratching, his face not indicating comprehension of any sort.

Only a few weeks remained until the fifth grade's trip to Gettysburg. That morning, Ms. Komplin directed her class in the making of hardtack, a staple of the soldier's diet. The teacher planned on baking enough of the hard, cracker-like squares for everyone to include in their field trip lunches, to eat on the bus on the way there. Students could also pack other items commonly eaten by soldiers, such as: bread with butter, jam, or honey; dried beef or jerky; hard-boiled eggs; carrot sticks or other veggies; cornbread; nuts; apples; and oatmeal cookies.

Ms. Komplin divided the class into groups to make the hardtack from flour, water, and salt. Naturally, she made sure that troublemakers Sully, Gonzo, and Breeze were all in different groups. Breeze measured the dry ingredients for his group, Gonzo added the water in his, and Sully helped stir his mixture, assisted by Vanessa.

"You sure we don't need some more water?" Sully asked because the stirring was slow going.

"I'm sure we got it right," replied the girl. She glanced around at the other groups; they seemed to be having just as much difficulty with the stirring. "I think it's supposed to be thick. Guess you gotta stir harder."

So he did. But his hard stirring caused flour to spit from the bowl, dusting up at them. Sully looked over at Vanessa's face and laughed. She looked at him and laughed too.

"A little less on yourselves, please," Ms. Komplin said as she handed the girl a towel.

Vanessa wiped her face; then she offered the towel to Sully before she realized his hands were also coated with flour. "I better do it," said the girl. She moved to wipe a cheek, but Sully took a step backward. "What? You don't trust me?"

It wasn't that. It was just…well…Sully had never let a girl touch him before. At least, not in a nice way. Until now, girls mostly tried to hurt him.

Embarrassed by his reflex to back away, Sully felt his face warming. "I'm too much of a mess," he tried to explain. "Maybe I should go…to the washroom. And dunk my head in the sink."

Vanessa laughed again. "If you want to. But let me at least get the bits outta your eyelashes. Wouldn't want the flour falling in your eyes, would you?"

Sully moved forward to let Vanessa dab at his closed eyelids. His head kept feeling warmer and warmer. Then he took the towel from her and rubbed the rest of his face.

"There's still some…around your nose," she said, pointing.

So he let Vanessa wipe him again. But as she did, Sully noticed Gonzo staring at him from across the room. He brushed the towel away.

Vanessa was surprised. "I thought you wanted me…"

"That's enough," he said gruffly.

After the hardtack mixtures were completely blended, students in each group spread their dough onto baking sheets and took them to the school kitchen for baking. Thirty minutes later, one student from each group returned to the kitchen to cut and turn the squares; they baked for another thirty minutes. After lunch, the hardtack had cooled and everyone got a sample to taste.

"Hard as rock," noted Gonzo as he clunked a square onto his desk.

"That's why they call it hardtack," explained Ms. Komplin.

"How'd they eat this stuff?" asked Sully. "I can't even bite into it. Breeze, you're lucky your jaws are wired."

"The soldiers did the best they could," answered the teacher. "Sometimes they put the hardtack in their morning coffee or in soup, to soften it."

"Man, no soldier should have to eat this!" said Gonzo.

"You're right, Carlos. But back then, they had little choice. Hardtack was one of the few foods that had a long shelf life. Stored in tins, it could last for years. And it was a quick way to fill a soldier's hungry stomach during a battle."

Ms. Komplin put all the hardtack they made into cookie tins and placed the tins on the side table. The squares would be distributed the morning of their trip. Then the students began to file out of the classroom for a lesson in the music room down the hall.

As he walked past the teacher's desk, Sully noticed that Ms. Komplin was again studying something in the left-hand drawer of her desk. What was it? He had no idea. Yet a tear—a single tear—was sliding down the woman's cheek.

In music class, Mr. Gorsham was repeating what he'd taught in their last lesson. "Every Good Boy Does Fine, representing E, G, B, D, and F, the notes on the five lines of the treble clef, from the bottom up."

Since Sully already had years of private piano lessons, Mr. Gorsham wasn't teaching him anything new. That was why he usually acted up in music class. But he missed the whoopie cushion the teacher took from him last month. What could he now do to amuse himself?

Yet Sully was also aware he needed to stay out of trouble. Because of his skyscraper. He knew Karmack was watching, but what if the creature needed to balance him and Gonzo both at the same time? Whose skyscraper would Karmack let fall?

No, it was too risky. Sully didn't dare try anything now.

But Gonzo had no such worry. While Mr. Gorsham was marking the treble clef lines on the board, the boy pulled a small bottle from his pocket. Inside was a stink bug. Gonzo placed the bug carefully on the shoulder in front of him. Then he squished the critter.

Vanessa felt Gonzo's knuckle press on her shoulder. She turned to the boy and whispered, "What're you doing?" Moments later, in a much louder voice, the girl cried, "Ewwww! What's that smell?"

The teacher spun around. "What's going on?"

Gonzo could barely contain himself. He put both hands over his mouth.

"Mr. Gorsham, I smell something awful!" said the girl with the squished bug on her shoulder. As everyone in Western Pennsylvania knows, stink bugs release the most terrible odor. Those near Vanessa were leaving their seats and moving to the other side of the room.

The teacher came over. "Oh, that *is* awful. Phew! Smells like a stink bug."

A step closer and Mr. Gorsham noticed the messy brown spot on the girl's shoulder. "Did you…? No, I don't imagine you did." The teacher looked at the others. Gonzo was the only one holding his mouth to suppress laughing noises. "Carlos, are you responsible for putting this stink bug on Vanessa's shoulder?"

Gonzo tried to shrug innocently, but he couldn't. The laughter was just too much—it burst forth from the boy.

"Uh-huh. Just as I suspected," said Mr. Gorsham. "Vanessa, go get a school T-shirt from your teacher to change into. Carlos, you come with me."

Sully knew Gonzo would be marched to the principal's office. Normally, he'd high-five the boy as he left; now he just shook his head.

When Vanessa returned to her classroom, Ms. Komplin was still crying. "Oh! Vanessa. What're you doing back?"

"I…got a stink bug on my blouse. Mr. Gorsham told me to change into a school T-shirt. But I don't know what that is." Bright yellow T-shirts had been distributed to students the year before, at the school's fiftieth anniversary celebration. Left-over shirts were still stored in some classrooms.

Ms. Komplin wiped her eyes. "In the closet," she pointed. "Just pick out your size."

Vanessa did. "What should I do with my top? It smells awful!"

The teacher reached into a lower drawer in her desk. "Put it in this plastic bag. Tie it nice and tight. Then place the bag outside the back door of the school until the day's over. Your mother will have to wash that smell out. Tell her to use lemon juice."

The girl paused. "Ms. Komplin? Were you…just crying?"

The teacher looked at her lap and sighed. "Can't stop thinking about my mother. She died…unexpectedly…in February. Before you joined our class."

"Oh. I'm so sorry."

"It was just…you know, so sudden. Still can't believe she's gone." The woman motioned toward her drawer. "I put her picture here, so I can look at it and smile. But I usually end up crying."

Vanessa touched the teacher's arm, saying, "Guess it takes time, to get over something like that." Ms. Komplin gave her an appreciative smile. Then Vanessa went to the washroom to change. She put her blouse in the plastic bag and placed it outside as Ms. Komplin had directed.

Sully grinned when he saw Vanessa in the bright yellow T-shirt. It read "High Five for Five-O" on the front and "Higgins Elementary" on the back. But he stopped smiling when she came near. She still smelled like stink bug. Luckily, there was only another hour of school left.

For Gonzo, there were two hours left; he'd received detention for the stink bug incident. Afterward, walking home by himself, he took his usual shortcut through the woods. And wouldn't you know, he came across a skunk. Normally these animals are nocturnal, roaming only at night; but this mother skunk had awakened early to forage for food.

Gonzo saw the skunk just a few feet ahead. He froze—one sudden move might induce the critter to spray. Gonzo didn't know it, but standing there beside him was Karmack, clutching a handful of ragweed pollen. The next moment, Karmack blew the pollen into Gonzo's face!

The boy couldn't stop himself. He had to sneeze. "Ahhh… choo! Ahhh…choo!"

Spooked, the animal immediately discharged her weapon. The spray shot in Gonzo's direction, completely smothering the boy in foul odor. It made him want to gag. It even burned his eyes. "Aaughhhhhh," Gonzo screamed as he sped toward home.

His mother had to draw him a bath with baking soda to remove the smell from his skin. As for his clothes, she had to burn those.

Yet this was nothing compared to what lay ahead. For Gonzo *and* Sully.

CHAPTER SEVENTEEN

Crunch Time

"A skunk?" Sully said with a laugh.

"A skunk," said Gonzo, clearly not laughing.

Breeze was cracking up too, although not much sound was coming from his wired jaws; mostly just, "Heh, heh, heh."

"Gonz, you must have the worst luck of anybody," said Sully. "But don't say I didn't warn you."

"You never warned me about a skunk!"

"I told you to watch what happened next time you pulled a prank. You squished that stink bug on Vanessa. And it boomeranged back on your stupid butt. Don't you get it?"

"You mean, because I made her stink…the skunk made *me* stink?"

"It's like that thing my dad always says—what goes around comes around."

"What's that supposed to mean?"

"The stuff you do comes back to you. Uma calls it karma."

Gonzo scratched his head. "It never happened like that before."

"Yeah but…lately it does."

Gonzo had to think about that.

"Remember last week," continued Sully. "You threw Logan Jensen's sneaker in the river; then a nail ripped your sneaker when you leaned against that fence, and when we crossed the bridge, that shoe fell off and went down into the river?"

"You mean, my sneaker dropped in the river 'cause I threw Jensen's sneaker there?"

"Yeah, exactly."

Breeze tried to smile, but with clenched teeth it only looked evil. He said, "What go awound, come awound."

"Just remember that," warned Sully, "next time you decide to do something stupid."

But on this day, Gonzo wouldn't remember.

Ms. Komplin spent the morning talking about the Underground Railroad and the trail runaway slaves used to travel through Pennsylvania to points north. Blairsville, the place the fifth grade would soon be visiting, was one of the known stops along the trail.

After the history lesson, Ms. Komplin reminded the class that, as always, they would be paired in the buddy system for their upcoming field trips. Students needed to choose a buddy to stay with the entire day. Vanessa turned in her seat to smile at Sully. He winked back at her.

Usually on field trips, Gonzo and Breeze alternated being Sully's buddy. It was Breeze's turn this time. But Sully hadn't told his friend he had another buddy in mind for this trip. Perhaps it slipped his mind.

At recess, Ms. Komplin led the class in drills as the students proudly marched across the schoolyard as a single military unit. As captain, Sully would be the one calling out the marching orders when they got to Gettysburg.

Allison Waters was their unit's flag bearer since her design was chosen for the class flag. Several students had worked with her to create the flag, which featured a large lump of coal with a gold crown resting on top. This was to signify King Coal, the natural resource that their part of Pennsylvania had so heavily relied on in the past; many area families had ancestors who once mined the coal. On either side of King Coal, the students drew colorful depictions of the state bird, Ruffed Grouse, and the state flower, Mountain Laurel.

"Company dismissed," Ms. Komplin finally said, allowing the class some free time before the end of recess.

Sully was laughing with Vanessa when Gonzo and Breeze came over to him. "My twurn for buddy," reminded Breeze.

"Uh, I forgot about that," said Sully. He looked at the girl. She seemed confused. Sully pulled her aside for a private chat. "Listen, Vanessa, I promised to buddy up with Breeze on our next field trip. But that was before I met you. Don't worry, I can handle this. I'll just convince Breeze he doesn't really want me for his buddy."

Sully planned on pretending he was getting a head cold. He knew that would work with Breeze. Then another thought—once Breeze backed out, Gonzo would step up as a replacement. How would he convince Gonz to back out too? Sully needed a minute to think. Then he remembered what Vanessa had told him about her uncle. There was the answer.

"Heheh," coughed Sully when he returned to his gang. "Heheck." He tried to sound more convincing the second time.

Breeze stared at him.

"Heheck. Must be coming down with my mom's cold."

"Your mwom's got a cold?"

"Yeah, musta picked it up from one of the babies." Sully's mom ran a daycare center.

Breeze looked terrified. "I can't ha a cold *now*, not wit dease wires on."

"Sure, I understand," said Sully. "I'll get me another buddy."

Gonzo stepped forward. "And that would be me."

"And you'd be right, Gonz. Under normal circumstances."

"Huh?"

"It's just that...well, Vanessa's uncle is a doctor. He gets medicine samples from the drug salesmen. He gave her one for colds and she swears it works. I'm sure she'll give me a sample if I...y'know, buddy up with her."

"You're gonna buddy with a *girl?*" Gonzo could hardly believe what he was hearing.

Sully shrugged. "I can't help it if she...likes me."

Gonzo pointed a finger at him. "You're turning into...a traitor!"

"No, I'm not. I just need that cold medicine."

"Yeah right." Gonzo waved a dismissive hand and started to walk away. "Be sure and kiss her too. And get lots of cootie germs."

Sully frowned. He didn't want to lose friends over this. He looked at Breeze, who was shaking his head. "What?" he asked.

"You diffwent now."

"I'm *what?*"

"Diffwent. You like *ghouls* now."

"Ghouls?"

"Yeah. Ghouls ike Anessa."

Sully started to feel defensive. Yet what Breeze said was true—he *did* like a ghoul (rather, a *girl*). And that *was* different. How could he punish Breeze for saying what he knew was true?

Gonzo, on the other hand, was not holding back his punches. He was mad—at Sully, for liking girls now. *What a dirty traitor*, thought Gonzo. He threw himself into the air and swung his fist. But when he came down, he landed against Bardo's backside.

"Heyyyyyy!" shouted Bardo. "What you think you're doing?"

Gonzo replied with a punch to the boy's belly. Bardo reeled backward and fell, hitting the concrete hard. "Owwwww, owwwww," he cried, rubbing the back of his head.

Sully heard Bardo's screams and feared the worst. He turned to see Gonzo running off. Could he catch him before…?

Too late! A skyscraper was about to topple!

As he rounded the corner of the school, Gonzo ran straight into an aluminum ladder left there by workers making repairs to the roof. He and the high ladder both wobbled.

Sully saw some flashes of light. Was it Karmack to the rescue?

But by the time Sully reached the side of the building, Gonzo was on the grass, his arms splayed out in front of him. Now the teetering ladder began to fall. It dropped in the direction of Gonzo's outstretched arms. The next thing Sully heard was a horrible bone-crunching sound.

The ladder had struck Gonzo on his left wrist. Amazingly, the boy had managed to save his right wrist by raising it into the air.

Yet only Sully could see what had actually happened—Karmack was holding up the arm.

CHAPTER EIGHTEEN
Friendship

"You didn't save Gonzo," Sully screamed at the top of his lungs. He and Karmack were in the woods again. Once the paramedics had arrived to treat his friend, Sully had taken off after the creature.

Karmack tried to explain. "I's can only hold…one hand at time."

"Man! I don't believe I trusted you. You failed me again!"

Karmack looked very sorry. "I's try very much best. Job no perfect. I's try."

Sully was still angry. Yet it *was* Gonzo's own fault. And hadn't Sully tried to warn him?

The boy plunked himself down on a nearby log. He put his elbows on his knees and rested his head in his hands. "Gonz just…wouldn't stay outta trouble. He just wouldn't."

Karmack nodded and took a seat next to the boy. "You's try help. I's see."

Sully let out a huge sigh. "Y'know, it all used to be so simple. Me and the guys, doing whatever we wanted. Anybody got in our way, we just clobbered 'em."

"Clobber no work, when you's grow up."

The boy turned and regarded the creature, who smiled up at him. "Grow up, huh? Not sure I'm ready for that. I liked my life just the way it was."

"All change, you's grow up."

Another thought occurred to Sully. "Hey, how come Gonz and Breeze don't understand about my liking Vanessa?"

"They's no be ready. For grow up."

"But I don't get it. They're the same age as me. Breeze and me even share the same birthday."

"Humans all grow…how say? Different on clock."

"Different on the clock? You mean…at different times?"

"Gotcha! Different times."

"But why?"

The creature shrugged its tiny shoulders and turned its palms upward. "No can say."

"You don't *know*? Or you just can't *say*?"

"I's only see what I's see—you's friends no be ready."

Sully nodded. Karmack's answer would have to suffice. "Guess my liking a girl means they won't be my friends anymore. Gonzo even called me a traitor."

"Friends come, go. Change. Some stay—you's friends, maybe."

"I dunno. Breeze and Gonzo seem kinda…boring lately. Maybe it's time for new friends."

"You's start new school. Get new friends. Gotcha?"

Sully grinned at the little guy. "Yeah, that's a gotcha all right."

The two sat there, quiet for a while, Sully reflecting on what lay ahead for him. Karmack waited patiently until the boy required another response.

Eventually Sully said, "Know what? You're a good listener, Karmack. I really like that about you."

The creature nodded. "I's be listener."

"And it's kinda nice, just coming here, talking things out with you."

"Gotcha."

"So you know what that makes you?"

Karmack didn't have a clue.

"My friend! Whattaya have to say to that?" But before the creature could answer, Sully said, "I know..."

"Gotcha!" they both said together.

CHAPTER NINETEEN
Fall from Grace

Gonzo had two broken bones in his wrist. The doctor had wrapped his arm in a cast and placed it in a sling; the boy returned to school the following week. But because he was left-handed, Gonzo couldn't write for the rest of the term. And he also couldn't punch.

It was now the day before the Blairsville field trip. That morning, Ms. Komplin passed out copies of the trip's itinerary along with maps of the walking tour of the town. After a quick review of the day's scheduled events, the teacher moved on to a discussion of what life was like for Civil War soldiers at Gettysburg.

Sully knew the bus ride to Blairsville would take about an hour. That didn't bother him—he'd be sitting next to Vanessa the whole way. As the teacher droned on about how tough life was at Gettysburg, Sully began to daydream. About him and Vanessa.

He saw the two of them sitting together on the bus, their hands by their sides. Then an accidental brush of the hands, resulting in an awkward moment. Next he imagined getting up the nerve to *take* her hand in his. Sully knew exactly how Vanessa would respond to that—she'd turn and smile at him. The way she always did. Then she'd probably say something like…

"Captain?" Ms. Komplin had raised her voice.

Sully snapped out of his reverie to see the teacher staring at him. "You…talking to me?"

"I am. But I expected a better response than that from a captain."

Sully blinked. He had no idea what the teacher was getting at. Vanessa said something under her breath to him. It sounded like "ice." So he said that.

"Ice?" repeated the teacher. A few students tittered. "You know the Battle of Gettysburg was fought in July, Curtis. How could the soldiers have problems with ice?"

"Oh," Sully said, thinking fast. "I meant to say, they didn't have *enough* ice." He heard more laughing.

"Well, I'm sure they didn't," replied Ms. Komplin. "I doubt they had any ice at all. There was no refrigeration back then." She turned to another student. "Noah, as the company's lieutenant, what kind of health problems do *you* think the men were dealing with at Gettysburg?"

With the teacher's attention now drawn away from them, Vanessa turned and rolled her eyes at Sully.

"Why'd you say *ice?*" he wanted to know.

"No, I said *lice.*"

"Oh." Sully's face was warm again, but not because of Vanessa. He'd been embarrassed in front of the whole class. Kids were laughing at what he'd said. They were laughing…at the Big Cheese. This was totally unacceptable.

"Vanessa," he whispered at the girl's back, "did you see who was laughing?"

"Huh?"

"Who was laughing when I said *ice?*"

She turned to him. "I dunno. Maybe Brayden. I couldn't tell, really. But I think Brayden might have laughed."

That was good enough. Brayden would be dealt with. Not with a punch, because that would only endanger Sully's skyscraper. But, oh yes, the boy would be dealt with!

When recess came, Sully bolted from his seat like a man possessed. He ran to Brayden's aisle and blocked the boy's exit.

" 'Scuse me," said Brayden, as he tried to squeeze past Sully.

"No, I won't excuse you," Sully said. He stood his ground.

"Well, get outta my way then."

Sully reached over, grabbed the boy's collar in one hand and put a fist in Brayden's face. "Don't you *ever* laugh when I say something. Hear me?" Fear shone in the boy's eyes.

Ms. Komplin, who was watching this display, now came over. "What is going on here?" She directed her question to the aggressor.

"Nothin'," Sully said as he released Brayden.

"Curtis, I'd like you to stay inside for recess today."

"Huh? Why?"

"Just stay," Ms. Komplin repeated.

They stood there until all the students had left. Then the teacher continued. "The others look up to you, Curtis, as their leader. That's why they elected you captain for our visit to Gettysburg."

Got that right.

"But…there are times when you don't set a good example for them. You sometimes threaten boys, like you did a minute ago with Brayden. That's not the way a good leader behaves. You can't continue to force respect out of them, Curtis. True leaders don't beat people into submission. Only dictators do that."

Sully didn't know what to say. Clobbering guys was the only way he knew of getting their respect. "Yeah, but…"

"There is no *yeah, but*. Not this time. I'm afraid I'm going to have to demote you until you learn how to be a good leader. Noah will take over as captain, and you'll be his lieutenant."

"Wait, you can't do that, Ms. Komplin. I *am* the class leader and everybody knows it."

"Leaders lead through good example, Curtis. And you're not showing good example. I've made up my mind. After recess, switch your captain's bars with Noah." She left him standing there.

Sully nearly collapsed to the floor. How could he live down this humiliation? It would ruin him! There had to be a way to change Ms. Komplin's mind. He glanced over at the teacher's desk, where the woman was once again looking at something in her side drawer. How could he convince her?

The intercom suddenly buzzed, requesting all fifth grade teachers to attend a quick meeting in the music room. Ms. Komplin immediately rose and left, leaving her drawer open. After she exited, Sully went to investigate.

There were the usual teacher items in the drawer, like pens, pencils, erasers, dry markers.

And some personal items too. He noticed the photo of a woman he assumed was her mother, positioned against the side of the drawer. Was this what kept drawing the woman's attention, he wondered?

Before he could investigate further, Ms. Komplin reappeared. She'd forgotten to take her notes for the field trip with her. She saw Sully looking into her drawer. She went over and slammed it shut. Sully heard the pens and pencils rattle inside.

"Get to your *own* desk," she ordered him.

Sully went to his desk and started to brood. He knew Ms. Komplin would announce his demotion right after recess. He'd be disgraced in front of the whole class—how could he stand that? The boy grew angrier with every passing minute.

When the students returned to their classroom, they saw Sully sulking at his desk. He looked angrier than they'd ever seen him before, and sometimes he looked downright furious.

As Ms. Komplin announced his demotion, Sully could feel everyone's eyes on him. He knew he'd lost their respect. But he decided to hold his head high, as high as any leader would. He wouldn't lower himself by meeting their eyes. *Or* the eyes of that evil Ms. Komplin!

And not only did the teacher make him and Noah switch their officer's bars, she also told them to create new ID badges, to reflect their change in rank. Now Sully's badge would broadcast to the world that he was just some lowly lieutenant, instead of proudly displaying his rightful position as captain. This would only add to the boy's humiliation.

Vanessa kept trying to catch Sully's eye. But he wouldn't look at the girl. He was too ashamed to look her way. And at lunchtime, Sully hid in the boys' washroom—he didn't want to deal with all the stares, whispers, and finger-pointing as word of his demotion spread throughout the cafeteria.

As he sat alone in the stinky washroom, ugly thoughts crept into Sully's mind. Ms. Komplin would have to pay for this. He'd make sure of it. Somehow he'd get her for this.

But...*how?*

CHAPTER TWENTY

Countdown to Leadership

The day had finally come. Everyone in Ms. Komplin's class was so looking forward to the field trip to Blairsville. For Breeze and Gonzo, the trip was a welcome diversion from the misery of having to live with broken bones. And even after his demotion, Sully was anticipating this day. Because he'd be spending it with Vanessa. It was the one thing that buoyed his spirits after his disgrace of the previous day.

But Ms. Komplin didn't look excited. Or even happy. Why was she scowling?

They'd find out soon enough.

"Quiet down, everyone," the teacher began. "I know you're all anxious to get to the bus and be on our way to Blairsville. But we have a grievous matter to settle first." She paused until the room became perfectly still. "Someone in this class has done something so awful, so…heartless…I can barely bring myself to talk about it."

She gazed out over the room, finding only a sea of astonished expressions. None of these students looked guilty. Ms. Komplin moved quickly to her desk and opened the side drawer. Withdrawing her photograph, she held it up for the class to see.

"This is a picture of my mother who, as you know, passed away recently. I keep it here in my desk drawer because it's… my favorite picture. And I can't get another copy. But… someone has defaced this picture. Ruined it. Turned it into a joke." She lowered her eyes and shook her head. "How one of you could…do such a thing…"

Students in the front seats were squinting to see what was wrong with the photo. It seemed to be just a normal picture of a woman. Then Stefan spotted something and pointed. This *was* a normal picture of a woman, but with…*a moustache.* Yes, a thin black line had been added to the upper lip of Ms. Komplin's dead mother!

Vanessa saw it and gasped. How could anyone do such a thing? She and others in the front began passing the information on to those behind them.

Ms. Komplin rested her bottom against the front of her desk, her arms folded. One hand still held a corner of the photo. "All right. I'd like the guilty party to come forward. Whoever's responsible for this brazen, cowardly deed needs to own up. We'll sit here until that happens."

No one moved a muscle. They were all in shock. *What about the field trip?* Just outside their classroom windows, three buses were lined up, their motors running while the drivers awaited their passengers.

Yet Ms. Komplin seemed resolute: no one would leave until the guilty party confessed. Kids began to look at one another, hoping the culprit might be shamed into coming forward.

Vanessa turned to Sully. She sheepishly pointed a questioning finger and raised her eyebrows. But the boy vigorously shook his head.

Other students soon directed their attention to Sully as well. He had a motive, didn't he? After all, hadn't Ms. Komplin just demoted him? They knew it was typical of Sully to take revenge for a slight. And wasn't he alone in the classroom when they all filed back after recess yesterday? That meant he had both motive and opportunity. And as for the means, a simple ballpoint pen would've got the job done.

Whispers around the classroom persisted. Ms. Komplin allowed the whispers, feeling peer pressure might indeed shame the villain. The teacher decided to get comfortable; this could take a while. She returned to her chair and began to busy herself with paperwork.

"Ms. Komplin?" asked a worried soul, rising from her desk.

"Yes, Lily?"

"Ms. Komplin, does this mean…we might not get to, you know…go to Blairsville, with the other fifth graders?"

"That's exactly what it means."

"Oh." Lily sat back down, looking even more worried.

Sully smiled to himself. If *he* were in charge, he'd find out who did this thing, in no time flat. All he had to do was shoot these punks one of his ferocious looks—that would get results.

Long minutes began to pass. The tension in the classroom rose. Everyone could feel it. Someone gulped. Then a girl began to sob. Soon other girls were sobbing too. Ms. Komplin ignored it all, keeping her eyes on her paperwork.

Those near the windows could see the other fifth graders boarding their buses. One bus was not boarding; it had to be theirs.

"Ms. Komplin," asked Gonzo, "couldn't we settle this thing tomorrow? I don't see why it has to be today."

The teacher sneered. "Oh, it has to be today, Carlos. The guilty party must realize how his or her selfish…and cruel…prank caused the rest of you to miss the field trip."

Gonzo looked right at Sully. Was that a snarl? Gonz had never looked at him like *that* before. Breeze seemed kind of mad too. So did wannabes all over the classroom. Sully wondered if he had any friends left.

One bus was pulling out of the school's driveway. Another was still loading. The driver of the third stood outside his bus, apparently puzzled by his missing passengers. He started walking toward the school's entrance.

Moments later, the intercom buzzed. It was the secretary in Principal Devers's office. "Ms. Komplin, is your class ready to board the bus yet?"

"We have a situation here," answered their teacher. "And it might end with *no one* boarding the bus!" She said this loud enough for the whole class to hear.

"Oh," said the secretary. "What should I tell the driver then?"

"Please ask him to wait just ten…no, fifteen…more minutes. If we aren't boarding by then, we aren't going."

Ms. Komplin heard gasps throughout the room. *Their teacher really meant it.*

"Geeze!" Noah said to the others. "Come *on* now. The guilty one's gotta stand up. 'Cause it just ain't fair to the rest of us."

Noah's words made Sully want to puke. *Some leader he is, whining like that. Real leaders don't whine.* Yet Ms. Komplin said true leaders didn't beat or threaten people either. But they never whine—Sully at least knew that.

"Here's a lesson for you," interjected Ms. Komplin, who looked right at Noah as she spoke. "As the new class leader, you must learn to deal with stressful situations like this."

"But…Sully's always been our leader," Noah said.

Got that right.

"Well," the teacher continued in a scornful voice, "*true leaders* set a good example. Whoever did this vile thing could never be a true leader."

Sully felt she was indicting him. And everyone was staring at him again.

Through the windows, the students watched their driver return to his bus. He went inside and took his seat; he turned the motor off. Just fifteen more minutes, their teacher had said.

"Please, whoever you are," a girl pleaded in between sobs, "just 'fess up, so we can go!"

But no one did. Ms. Komplin went back to her paperwork; she appeared unruffled by the growing agony in her classroom.

More minutes passed. How much longer could Sully bear this torment? He knew everyone thought he was the culprit. Gazing around the room, he saw angry faces on boys, despairing ones on girls. Vanessa's was the most painful to see—she looked as if she'd lost her best friend in the whole world.

"It's not fair," sobbed Abigail. Then she kicked Sully's butt through the opening in his seat. That only riled the boy. He swung around and put an angry fist in her face. But she was too upset to care. "Oh, why don't you just grow up?!" she cried.

Grow up? Isn't that what Karmack said was happening to him—he was growing up? So how come Abigail said this to him? *Wasn't* he growing up?

Hmmm. Sully began to reflect on his behavior. Threats accompanied by a fist to the face—that was an old habit, and one he always relied on. But like Karmack said, maybe this wouldn't work anymore. Ms. Komplin certainly didn't think so. Maybe he needed to try something new. *But what?*

More minutes passed. Someone watching the classroom clock began a countdown. "Only eight more minutes."

Sully was thinking hard. *What to do, what to do?* If he didn't find a solution soon, the whole class would miss out on the field trip. And they'd all blame *him*, even thought he wasn't the one who defaced Ms. Komplin's picture. But was there a way for Sully to regain their respect without losing their trust?

Vanessa was squirming in her seat. Sully wanted to say something to the girl, but he wasn't sure what would help. Did *she* at least believe he was innocent?

He tapped her on the shoulder. When Vanessa turned her head, Sully said, "It's not me, I didn't do it. And…I wouldn't lie to you. Honest."

The girl closed her eyes and nodded slightly before turning back around. What did that mean, Sully wondered?

The clock-watcher said, "Five more minutes."

What would make these punks respect me again? Being tough always worked before. But it wouldn't this time. He knew that now. Sully looked back at his friends. They still seemed angry. He knew they'd never forgive him if they couldn't go on this field trip. Breeze had endured so much with his wired jaw, and Gonzo's wrist was giving him a lot of discomfort.

The seconds continued to tick by. Pretty soon, the clock-watcher begged, "Come on! There's only three minutes left!" But what could Sully do? Or what could he say to make the guilty party come forward? That's when it hit him—there was nothing he could do or say to make someone else take the blame. Nothing.

With just over a minute remaining, Sully stood up. He'd reached a decision. He said simply, "I did it."

The teacher put down her pen and smiled victoriously. "All right, everyone. Gather up your things and head out to the bus. Stefan, you run ahead to tell the driver we're coming." The boy didn't need to be told twice; off he flew. Then she said, "Curtis, you come with me."

Vanessa shot Sully a despairing look as he got up from his desk to follow Ms. Komplin to the principal's office.

But Uma just sighed and said, "Karma."

CHAPTER TWENTY-ONE

Go Poof!

"Curtis, I'm really disappointed in you," said Principal Devers. "Of all the stunts you've pulled over the years, this has got to be the worst."

Sully looked at the hands in his lap. What could he say? It *was* a terrible thing to deface his teacher's photo. But he was the only one who seemed to know he'd never do such a thing.

"Do you have anything to say for yourself?"

Still looking down, Sully shook his head.

"All right. Instead of going to Blairsville with your class, you'll spend the day here, assisting my secretary."

Still no reaction from the boy.

"What you did was more than just mean, Curtis. You went into your teacher's desk and removed a personal item; then you deliberately disfigured that item. You know, don't you, that it's against the law to vandalize someone's property?"

Now the boy looked up. There was fear in his eyes.

"Don't worry; I'm not going to call the police. But your punishment must be harsher than usual. I've decided to cancel your trip to Gettysburg. I'll arrange for you to do community service over the three days your class will be there."

Sully's mouth dropped open. "Principal Devers, please don't do this!"

"I'm sorry, Curtis. But you've got to learn a lesson this time. Denying you this trip is the only thing I can think of…"

"Look, I'll stay after school—every day, til the end of the year. I'll do anything you want. Just *please* let me go on the Gettysburg trip! *Please!*"

The principal closed his eyes and shook his head. "I'll refund your parents's money."

Sully felt like he'd been stabbed through the heart. The fifth grade overnight! The one thing every kid looked forward to as reward for making it through Higgins Elementary. Now it was being taken from him.

As directed, the boy spent the morning in the office, assisting the secretary. He didn't mind the work, mostly sorting and filing papers. But his mind kept drifting to what he was missing at Blairsville—especially being with Vanessa. And since she was left without a field trip buddy, Ms. Komplin probably forced the girl to buddy up with her. He felt sorry for that.

At recess time, the secretary said Sully could go outside with the other students. She also asked the boy to take some papers to put in the recycling container out back.

Sully did as requested, depositing the papers in the large rubber trash barrel marked RECYCLING, which stood next to the open dumpster. Then he noticed flashes of light buzzing all around him. Karmack was there. The creature stopped long enough to motion Sully toward the woods. Eager for sympathetic company, the boy followed.

When they reached the clearing, Sully was surprised to see Karmack jumping up and down in excitement. "You's do, you's do," the creature shouted.

"Huh? What'd I do?"

"Make skyscraper go *poof!*"

"It went poof? Really? That whole pile over my head?"

Karmack stopped jumping to nod its little head. "Go *poof!*"

"But…*how?*"

"You's find shortcut!"

"I did?"

"Shortcut make skyscraper go *poof.*"

"I don't get it. What was the shortcut?"

"You's hurt you's, so make all happy!"

Sully rubbed his chin. "You're saying, I hurt myself and that made everybody else happy?"

"No, you's *take* hurt to *give* happy. All happy now."

The boy scowled. "Happy? I don't think so, Karmack. Ms. Komplin and Principal Devers think I did a rotten thing, Vanessa no longer trusts me, Gonzo and Breeze feel betrayed, and the rest of the guys want a new leader. Nobody's happy. Especially me."

Karmack smiled at him. "You's give happy away, so all can be happy. But you's be happy too—you's see! Big Cheese again!"

Sully couldn't imagine how he could ever be the Big Cheese again. Not after what everyone now believed about him.

The creature resumed its dancing. "Job done. All be balance. I's go."

"You're going?"

"All be balance."

Sully felt a tinge of regret. Despite all the problems this creature had caused, he'd still miss talking to the little guy. "Where will you go?"

"I's go where sent."

"Will I ever see you again, like…here in the woods?"

"No can say. If new skyscraper, I's job be balance."

"Yeah, okay. I get that." Sully turned to walk away but suddenly stopped. "I just…wanna say…y'know, thanks."

"I's no save, *you's* save."

Apparently, Sully *had* saved himself. And yet…without Karmack's help—especially to explain things—could he have pulled it off? He wasn't sure. But this much Sully *did* know—this little dude was all right. "Maybe I did save myself. But you helped, Karmack."

"I's help?"

"You explained about the skyscraper, and how it had to be balanced. If you hadn't done that, I mighta ended up like my friends."

Karmack nodded. "Dreadful, awful doom."

"Yeah. But you led me away from all that. Hey, that makes *you* a leader. Like the Big Cheese."

This made the creature crack up. "I's be Big Cheese? Hah! That great funny."

"Okay, I *gotcha* then." Sully stuck out his hand despite knowing what the creature might do with it. "Guess this is goodbye, Karmack. Take care of yourself, dude. Don't let some hurricane blow you out to space."

The little guy did as Sully expected, spitting in the boy's hand. "You's take care too. No make skyscraper."

Sully smiled as he wiped his hand along the side of his pants. "Don't worry—*I's no make skyscraper.*" Then with one final wave, "So long, Karmack."

The creature waved too before it sped off through the woods, moving faster and faster until all that remained were tiny flashes of light.

CHAPTER TWENTY-TWO

Schoolyard Terror

As Sully slowly retreated from the woods, he thought he heard some screams up ahead. They seemed to be coming from the kids in the schoolyard. Yet these were not screams of happy children at play. They were shouts of terror.

When he reached the schoolyard, Sully saw children running in every direction. A first grader was clutching his ankle and crying; spots of blood were on his pant leg. Just next to the boy, a playground monitor was wildly swinging her purse at something. Sully sped up to investigate.

From about twenty feet away, he could finally see what was at the center of the ruckus—a raccoon. But not your typical raccoon—this critter was drooling and baring its pointed teeth. *Rabid*. And he knew what that meant: a wild animal infected with rabies would attack anything that moved, and wouldn't stop until it was finally subdued.

The playground monitor kept swinging her purse, but the raccoon continued to lunge at her. Sully came up from behind. The woman turned to find him standing there beside her. She gave him a little nod, grateful to have the assistance of the oldest boy in the yard. "I don't think…" she told him, "…this purse will hold him off for long."

Sully agreed. The raccoon's jerky movements and the wild look in its eyes confirmed that this animal was not in its right mind.

Positioned a few feet from the back entrance of the school, the raccoon was preventing anyone from getting in or out of the building. Sully knew they had to get the critter far enough away so the kids could run inside to safety.

Principal Devers appeared from around the corner of the building. He was running. When he reached Sully and the playground monitor, still swinging her purse, he abruptly stopped. "The animal control people are on their way," he told them.

"That's good," the woman replied, "but what'll we do 'til then?"

"If only…there was some way," said the principal, "to contain the animal, until they get here."

Contain—this word suggested something to Sully. Of course! He'd placed papers in the recycling *container* next to the dumpster. Now *there* was an idea!

Sully reached over to take the handle of the purse from the monitor. "Can I borrow this?"

"Well…sure." She let go.

The boy took over swinging the purse at the animal. "I'm gonna try and get the raccoon over to the dumpster," he told them. "And when I do, you get the kids inside."

"It's too dangerous," the principal said. "That animal's fast and his teeth are sharp. We better stay put until the animal control people arrive."

"No way," said Sully. "It'll bite more kids before they get here."

The raccoon was now standing on its hind legs, pawing viciously at the swinging purse. Sully took a step backward, hoping the animal would follow him. The raccoon rushed forward. Both the principal and the playground monitor instinctively jumped out of the way.

Yet Sully remained calm, taking another backward step, then another, all the while keeping a cautious eye on the animal in case it suddenly charged him. Gradually, Sully picked up his pace as the raccoon continued to follow. When the boy reached the corner of the building, he saw the principal and the monitor corralling the kids. Now they would be safe!

As the raccoon turned the corner behind him, Sully decided to make a run for the dumpster. He dropped the purse and took off. The raccoon scampered after him. Sully made a flying leap at the dumpster, grabbing its rim and scrambling up its side. Knowing the raccoon would be on him in seconds, the boy pulled himself up to the narrow ledge at the top. He squatted on the ledge and steadied himself against the joint of the dumpster's attached lid.

The raccoon was now at the foot of the dumpster, clawing its way up the side of the bin. Sully carefully inched along the back ledge until he reached the other side of the dumpster. Just below him was the recycling container on the ground. He reached down to grab it; his idea was to drop the container over the animal. But the receptacle was heavy with paper. Sully couldn't even lift it.

The raccoon stared at Sully from the opposite rim. The boy now realized he had to get the animal into the dumpster, and to do that he'd have to go in first. So he jumped into the trash heap, keeping one hand firmly on the rim. When he saw the raccoon jump in at the other end, Sully turned and scrambled back up the side of the bin. As he did, he felt the raccoon's claws scratching at his jeans.

When he reached the top, Sully squatted on the ledge as before and looked down into the dumpster. The raccoon lunged up at him but fell. For the moment at least, the critter seemed contained.

Sully jumped down from the dumpster to find Principal Devers sprinting toward him. Together, they lifted the heavy lid of the dumpster and slammed it down.

When the animal control officers arrived, the principal told Sully he could leave for the day. After all, he'd done enough.

Sully was glad to go home early. He certainly didn't want to be around when the field trip buses returned—seeing all those happy faces would only make him gag.

After gathering up his things, Sully stepped from his classroom with his backpack. But to his surprise, the hallway was filled with kids. First graders, second graders, even third and fourth graders. And when they saw him, they all began to cheer. Sully didn't know what to do.

Principal Devers stepped forward. "You're their hero," he told the boy.

Sully's face flushed. He could feel it. "I just did…what anyone woulda done."

The principal laughed his hearty laugh. "No, you did what a *brave* someone would've done. We're proud of you, Curtis. You're one brave boy."

The students continued to clap as Sully left the building. He waved and smiled, but just a little.

* * * *

When the field trip buses arrived back, Principal Devers was there to welcome everyone. He just loved hearing firsthand about the students' experiences. And when the principal saw Ms. Komplin, he asked her to stop by and see him before she left for the day.

So she did. Principal Devers then recounted the story of the rabid raccoon and how Sully had saved the day.

Ms. Komplin shook her head in disbelief. "Curtis Sullenburg—the boy who defaced my mother's photograph?"

"The same. And I saw him with my own eyes—on top of the dumpster, trapping that vicious creature."

The teacher continued to shake her head. "The boy with eleven detentions last month."

"Uh-huh. And if he hadn't acted, who knows how many more children would've been bitten?"

"Curtis. Curtis Sullenburg."

"Yup. Saved the day."

As she walked out of the principal's office, the woman was still shaking her head.

Once back in her classroom, Ms. Komplin opened the left-hand drawer of her desk. There lay the photo of her mother, with the added moustache. It made her shudder.

Curtis—the boy who rescued everyone from the rabid raccoon—did this thing. How could it be that the hero of the day was also the heartless vandal who ruined her most prized possession?

She lifted the picture and rubbed at the inked-on moustache as if this would make it disappear.

But…wait a minute! It *was* disappearing! She rubbed some more. And soon the moustache was gone. Ms. Komplin blinked several times. She'd been so sure that someone—particularly someone named Curtis Sullenburg—had inked on this moustache. But it couldn't have been ink.

She rummaged around in the drawer. And there she found the eyebrow pencil she'd misplaced a few weeks earlier. Its cap was off. Ms. Komplin took the eyebrow pencil and traced a delicate line across her mother's top lip. It looked just like the previous line. Then she rubbed it off again.

The teacher sat down in her chair. What had she done? She suddenly felt sick to her stomach.

CHAPTER TWENTY-THREE

Worthy Captain

The next day, Sully arrived late to school—he still wasn't eager to hear everyone talking about their wonderful experiences at Blairsville. And by the time he reached his classroom, Ms. Komplin was already making her morning announcements. He figured he'd probably get detention again.

"Mr. Sullenburg, how nice of you to join us," his teacher said with a wicked smile.

Man, I'm in for it.

But before Sully could take his seat, Ms. Komplin said to him, "Step outside with me."

Out in the hallway, the woman stopped just beyond the door. "I want you to tell me something, Curtis. Why'd you do it?"

What did she want him to say—that he hated her so much he decided to ruin the photo of her dead mother?

"Look Ms. Komplin, I know you won't believe me, but I didn't draw that moustache. I said I did, but I really didn't. I could never do that. And I don't know who did."

"I know you didn't do it."

The boy had to shake his head to make sure he heard her right. “You *know?*”

“I do now. So tell me why you took the blame.”

Sully didn’t know how to respond. “Well, what choice did I have? Everyone just assumed it was me. Maybe…on accounta all the pranks I pulled, in the past.”

“But you could’ve just kept your mouth shut.”

“And ruin the trip for everyone? No one was standing up, admitting they’d done it. We were running outta time. I had to do something.”

“So…you didn’t want everybody to have to suffer?”

“Well, that didn’t seem right. I’m sorry I lied to you. But I had to do *something*.”

The teacher smiled at him, this time not so wickedly. “Curtis, I misjudged you. And for that, I’m truly sorry.”

Sully looked down. “ ’Sokay…I guess.”

“No, it’s not okay. But I’m going to try and make it okay.” She turned for the door. “Let’s go back inside.”

After Sully took his seat, Ms. Komplin hushed everyone to make another announcement.

“Class, I…have a confession to make. Yesterday, I jumped to a very bad conclusion.” The teacher opened her top drawer and once more removed her photograph. “I thought someone had drawn a moustache on my mother’s picture here, and I was deeply hurt by that. But what I thought was a moustache was only a mark made by my eyebrow pencil. The cap must’ve come loose when I slammed the drawer shut, and the pencil touched up against the photo. It made a harmless little line, which easily rubbed off. See?” She held up the photo. Those in the front seats nodded their heads.

“But I assumed, as did you all, that Curtis was responsible for ruining my photo. He wasn’t. Yet he took the blame and suffered the consequences.”

The teacher paused to allow that information to sink in. Soon whispered exclamations were spreading throughout the room.

Her head bowed, Ms. Komplin began to pace in front of her desk. "Class," she said, "this…incident…teaches us an important lesson in leadership. A true leader is someone who puts others before himself, never hesitating to sacrifice his own needs and wants for theirs. I believe this is what we witnessed here yesterday. A true leader rose up from your class, and put our needs and wants before his own."

She paused again but continued to pace. Sully felt his face warming. Then Ms. Komplin resumed, "This leader knew how much the field trip meant to all of us, and how painful it would be for us to miss it. And this seemed more important than any punishment he might have to suffer." The teacher suddenly stopped in front of Vanessa's desk. She motioned toward the boy sitting behind her. "Class, here is someone who knows what it takes to be a true leader. And a hero. Yesterday, while we were on the field trip, he saved a yard full of children from a rabid raccoon."

Everyone's eyes bulged. Vanessa turned to smile at the hero.

Ms. Komplin concluded, "Curtis Sullenburg, I hereby reinstate you as captain of this unit." For a brief moment, there was no further sound in the room. Then somewhere in the back a boy shouted, "Way to go, Sully."

Breeze stood up. And started to clap. Everyone else stood up and did the same. Even Bardo. Gonzo clapped his good hand against the cast on his wrist.

Everyone was clapping. And Sully hadn't punched or threatened any of them.

"Speech," someone shouted. And everyone repeated the word until all were chanting, "Speech, speech, speech…"

Sully looked at Vanessa, and she was smiling at him. The biggest, most beautiful smile he'd ever seen. "You gotta say something," she told him.

But *what?* Sully realized he couldn't afford to pass up this opportunity. Yet what do you say when everyone thinks you're a hero? He might be the Big Cheese again, but he didn't want to say anything *too* cheesy.

Still not knowing what he'd say, Sully stood up. The students were on their feet, so he stepped up on his desk chair to get above them. "Uh…thanks," he began. "And thanks too, Ms. Komplin, for those nice words." He paused, still not sure what they wanted or expected to hear from him. Then something came to mind. Words from an old movie—a western—where the hero shuffled his feet and said: *Aw, shucks…I ain't no hero. Anyone coulda done what I done.* So Sully said that.

All at once, everyone erupted into laughter. It caught Sully by surprise.

"But what about taking the blame for the picture?" asked Vanessa. "So the rest of us wouldn't miss the field trip?"

"Well, that." More words from the western came to mind. "I just wanted…a day off from seeing your ugly mugs!" Everybody laughed again.

And the next moment, the strangest thing of all happened. Sully looked out at the sea of smiling faces and smiled *back*—something he told Karmack tough guys never did.

CHAPTER TWENTY-FOUR

No More Skyscrapers

After Ms. Komplin explained to Principal Devers about her mistake and how Sully nobly took the blame for it, the principal did an about-face. He immediately reversed his cancellation of Sully's trip to Gettysburg.

So the entire fifth grade went on the three-day field trip to the historic Military Park. They were fortunate to have perfect weather those three days, and everyone seemed to thoroughly enjoy the trip. Especially Sully, who had buddied up with Vanessa.

While walking one of the ranger-led tours of the Park, Gonzo noticed Sully's hand sliding toward Vanessa's. And before he knew it, the two were actually holding hands. Not only that, Sully had the silliest grin on his face.

Gonzo felt sick to his stomach. He poked Breeze and motioned ahead of them, at the hand-locked couple.

"Awwwgh!" the boy said through his wired, clenched teeth. "Coodies!"

"What's happening to Sul?" wondered Gonzo.

Overhearing, Uma whispered, "It's karmic."

"Huh?"

"Your friend, he is reaping the rewards of karma. Sully is getting what he deserves for something good he did."

Gonzo looked over at Breeze, who seemed as confused as he was. "Something...*good? Sully?*"

"Yes. Perhaps it was saving the children from the raccoon," said Uma.

"Or," Breeze suddenly agreed, "takin da blame for da moustache."

"Of course," Uma replied. "He is a hero on both counts, isn't he?"

Gonzo continued to look bewildered. This sure was a different Sully. Then he shrugged. Maybe he could get used to the new one. After all, Sully was still the toughest kid he knew.

* * * *

On the last day of school, the usual ceremony for the graduating fifth graders was held in the auditorium. Awards were presented to those who excelled in academic subjects, which also included Art, Music, and Creative Writing. In addition, honors were bestowed on several fifth graders exhibiting qualities of good citizenship, and those with perfect attendance records.

The very last award was a special one. Unlike the others, which were printed on parchment paper, the Award for Exceptional Bravery was a small wooden plaque with a gold plate. The name Curtis Sullenburg was engraved on it.

Principal Devers shook Sully's hand as he gave the boy the plaque. Again the students clapped, and Sully's own class cheered. Even Bardo.

After the ceremony, the fifth graders returned to their classrooms to say their goodbyes. Ms. Komplin insisted on dismissing the students individually, allowing each to choose between a hug and a handshake. The girls mostly wanted hugs while the boys opted for handshakes.

When it came Sully's turn, he hesitated. Ms. Komplin smiled and said, "C'mere." Then she grabbed up the toughest kid in all of Higgins Elementary. Sully had no choice but to hug her back, at least a little. "You're the noblest boy I know," she whispered in his ear. "And I'm not talking about the raccoon incident."

Sully pulled back and looked at the teacher's face. *She really meant it.*

Minutes later, Principal Devers echoed Ms. Komplin's sentiments as he stopped Sully in the hallway. "I hope you'll come back and visit us, Curtis. A hero like you is always welcome at Higgins Elementary."

Sully wasn't used to such nice treatment from the adults at his school. Particularly from the principal. "Uh…sure," he mumbled.

Vanessa caught up to him and smiled. Then she asked Sully if maybe he'd like to see a movie together. Sometime over the summer.

Sully felt his face warming. "O…kay, I guess."

"Just gimme a call," she said while holding two fingers next to her face in the familiar phoning gesture. Her other hand held out a slip of paper with a telephone number on it.

"Great," said the boy as he took the paper. "Guess I'll be seeing you then."

"You'll be seeing me *soon*," Vanessa corrected him. She gave him one more smile before skipping off.

You can count on it. Sully was still grinning when Breeze and Gonzo reached him.

"You wook…happy," said Breeze.

"Prob'ly glad to be leaving," Gonzo added. "Am I right, Sul?"

Their leader switched to his fierce look. "Time we blew this joint."

The three boys bounded out of the school. But once outside, they had to dodge students shoving each other in the bus lines.

"Hey, watch it!" Sully glowered at the first grader who'd smashed into him. Seeing it was the Big Cheese, the boy froze. But Sully just winked at the kid and continued on.

When they reached the end of the driveway, Uma was there, waiting to cross the street. She asked if she could see Sully's award. He handed it to her.

"My, my. So very special. Your parents will be very proud."

Sully took it back with a grunt. He didn't want anyone thinking the plaque meant anything to him.

"This award?" Gonzo asked Uma. "Is it…karmic too?"

"Oh yes," the girl replied. "Another reward for a good deed, well done."

"Karmic, huh?" asked Sully. He smiled to himself. *More like…Karmack.*

As the crossing guard waved them on, the group of students walked to the other side of the road. Sully suddenly stopped. Looking back at the school, the boy sensed he was leaving a large part of his childhood behind.

It was probably just…skyscrapers.

ABOUT THE AUTHOR

J.C. Whyte

J. C. Whyte discovered a love for writing while she was still in elementary school. Back then of course, she only wrote children's stories. But when she grew up, J. C. had to face the harsh reality that such writing seldom pays the bills. So she got her degrees in Journalism and Communications, and turned to Public Relations, where for ten years she focused her creative energies in feature writing.

Then after marriage, kids, several more degrees and occupations (including stints as a travel agent and paralegal), J. C. entered law school. While there, she became a columnist for the student newsletter; one of her humorous articles was even published in *The National Jurist*.

After graduating and passing the Bar, J. C. realized within a few years that creative writing was still what made her heart sing. So now, as a grandma, she has returned to writing for children. And with the publication of *Karmack*, she's come full circle, back to where her writing journey truly began!

Did you enjoy Karmack? If so, please help us spread the word about J.C. Whyte and MuseItUp Publishing. It's as easy as:

•Recommend the book to your family and friends
•Post a review
•Tweet and Facebook about it

Thank you
MuseItUp Publishing

MuseItUp Publishing
Where Muse authors entertain readers!
https://museituppublishing.com
Visit our website for more books for your reading pleasure.

You can also find us on Facebook:
http://www.facebook.com/MuseItUp
and on Twitter:
http://twitter.com/MusePublishing

CPSIA information can be obtained at www.ICGtesting.com
Printed in the USA
BVOW08s0140170516

448379BV00001B/7/P